YOU GLOW
IN THE DARK

YOU GLOW IN THE DARK

Liliana Colanzi

*Translated from the Spanish by
Chris Andrews*

LONDON

For Ed

'The mountain flows, the river sits still.'
Dōgen

Contents

The Cave	1
Atomito	13
The Debt	39
Chaco	51
The Greenest Eyes	63
The Narrow Way	69
You Glow in the Dark	83
Note	105

The Cave

1

She tripped and fell; her swollen belly hit the ground. She hadn't seen the rock. The rabbit carcass tumbled over the snow, spattering it with crimson specks. The young woman dragged herself to the cave. Something had broken inside her and was coming out between her legs. She howled her pain: the bats came streaming out over her head.

She had begun to swell up several moons after a feast to which the men of another clan had been invited. She didn't know who had got her pregnant, nor did she care. What she cared about was being a smart hunter and a fast runner, and everyone knew that females with a burden were slower and sure to get left behind, so they had to stay at the settlement until it was time to give birth.

The pain threw her onto her back. She tried to remember what women did in this situation. In her mind's eye she could see her mother crouched over, squeezing thin, bluish babies out onto the ground. They always died a few days later. Only she and her sister, who were strong and skilled at clinging to life, had managed to survive. She rolled up to a squat and immediately felt the urge to push. She shouldn't have left the settlement swollen up like that, but it was boring to stay back with the old women while the young ones were out in a band, on the trail of bison.

So she had slipped out and gone to check a trap that she had made with pine branches a while back: she found the rabbit trembling, caught between the branches, and felt an innocent joy as she slit its throat.

Pleased with herself, she had failed to see the rock, and because of that stupid carelessness, she was shedding her lump ahead of time and without any help. Luckily it was already sliding out between her legs: a damp salamander. She was groping for it when a spasm of pain bent her double. Another lump . . . ! The second baby dropped out beside the first. She fell forwards onto her elbows, exhausted, and used her knife to sever the purple entrails connecting her to the newborn creatures.

She raised their sticky bodies, one in each hand: a male and a female, their little arms reaching out to her, streaked with delicate, branching veins. Numb with cold but flushed from the effort, confused in her exhaustion, she gazed at them, intrigued. Something terrible had just happened to her, something the old women discussed in whispers around the fire: she had given birth to double children. This was an unmistakable sign of her wrongdoing. The tiny, identical, hungry mouths attached themselves to her nipples, and the sucking – pleasurable and painful at once – relieved her engorged breasts.

A coyote sang in the distance: night was coming at a gallop. She had survived the lump, as she had previously survived gomphotheres, cold, hunger and fever. The instinct for life stirred within her again, alert and sharp. Gusts of snow blew in between the icicles, reminding her that there was no time to waste. She removed the babies from her nipples and took them into the light to contemplate them once again: they were almost translucid, and covered with the finest down. She carried them to the back of the cave and, moved by curiosity or playfulness, pressed the four little soles of those bloody feet on the wall and, beside them, the palms of her own dirty hands. The symmetry of the prints on the rock gave her a sense of achievement. Then, with the same clean stroke that she had applied to the rabbit, she slit the throats of the double children. Before the darkness covered them, they let out a soft mewing.

She stepped out of the cave, no lump now, and ran off across the snowy steppe.

2

One night a twenty-two-year-old food worker by the name of Xóchitl Salazar got lost in a thunderstorm on the way back to her village after working at a tamale stand in Guelaguetza. Disorientated in the darkness and terrified by the lightning bolts zigzagging across the sky like varicose veins, she ended up in the cave. From there she tried to call her boyfriend, who hadn't wanted her to work at that fiesta. There was no signal on her mobile phone, but the blue glow of the torch app dispersed the hungry shadows.

What she saw imprinted itself on her retina: the wall at the back was covered with rudimentary paintings, composing a complicated prehistoric fresco. The images were superimposed; it was clear that they had been added by different artists over centuries. They scared her: the set of figures revealed a forbidden order, a heresy. The animals were out of proportion with the humans. Some were as big as a hippopotamus or an elephant, although no one had ever seen a hippopotamus or an elephant in Oaxaca. And the postures of the human figures suggested scenes of – she crossed herself twice – group sex. She placed her hand on the print that another hand had left on the rock: the shape of her palm exactly matched the outline.

It was almost dawn by the time the rain stopped and Xóchitl Salazar was able to make her way home across the fields in her wet, muddy dress with the news of her discovery. But she didn't get the chance to say a word. Her boyfriend, sick with jealousy, was waiting behind the door with a baseball bat. She hardly felt the blow. She fell to the ground face up, with her forehead caved in, and the image of those strange animals fixed in her pupils.

3

The light rose out of the depths of the night unseen by any living creature. A silvery flame the size of a ring, sprung from nothing. It stopped in the middle of the cave, floated there, and suddenly expanded to several times its original size. Within it there appeared the outline of a chrysalis composed of water or some other quivering substance. The chrysalis spun on its axis, unhurriedly at first, then at great speed, until the cave became a capsule of vibrating light. A toad croaked; from the village came the sound of songs in honour of the Thunder God.

Lowering itself out of the flame, the chrysalis descended to the cave floor. The light began to fold in on itself, shrinking to a speck; the toad leaped up and swallowed it. On the ground now, the chrysalis convulsed. Its lips opened like the mouth of a dying fish; with every spasm it belched a shower of particles into the night air. And when it had emptied itself, it fell apart.

The particles the chrysalis had flung into the air rose up and adhered to the roof of the cave, where they were broken down by fungi or devoured by hibernating bats. Over the years, a mutation developed in the mouths and noses of those bats, which enhanced their capacity to capture soundwaves and thereby locate insects. The plagues that had previously ravaged the fields of the nearby village, causing famine and fatal diseases, came to an end.

From that point on, the harvests increased, and as time went by the village became the centre of a small and flourishing empire: its textiles and earthenware, original in their form and design, came to be known among the farthest-flung communities. The villagers also began to try out a syllabic writing system based on glyphs, which they used to recount how humans were directly descended from trees.

This prosperity provoked the envy of the neighbouring peoples. One night, while the villagers were sleeping it off after long and rowdy revelry to glorify the Thunder God, an enemy army laid siege to the village. The men were killed or sacrificed to other gods, the women taken into slavery, and the houses and temples burned down to their foundations. Within a few years nobody remembered the settlement or its inhabitants. All that survived of that fleeting civilisation were the textiles, kept alive by the slave women and absorbed into the conquering culture.

The mutant bats survived for several hundred years, gathering into a bunch of little mouths and pointed ears at the vertex of that cave throughout the winter months. Over time they were able to displace other species of bats. At the end of the sixteenth century, however, they were wiped out suddenly by a virus that came from Europe in the nose of a Dominican friar sent to try a group of Zapoteco Indians for heresy. The man stopped to take a nap in the shade of the cave and never knew the consequences of the sudden sneeze that woke him up: in his dream he had been walking through the cool courtyards of his monastery in Caleruega as the sun set over the rose bushes.

Weeks later the floor of the cave was carpeted with hundreds of bat skeletons, delicate as pine needles. The unusually heavy July rains ended up washing them away.

4

The centuries of the mutant bats were prosperous for the cave as well. The bat guano, made up of insect exoskeletons, sustained life in the half-light. Beetles laid their eggs in it, and their larvae – hungry, ancestral miniatures – found refuge in the shit. Sunk in that dark matter, they traversed the inky night of their metamorphosis to emerge in their definitive form. Diligent colonies of fungi and bacteria worked on the excrement, breaking it down, before being devoured by the Coleoptera. Attracted in turn by the beetles, salamanders hid in the cracks of the rock.

This whole world collapsed with the sudden disappearance of the bats. As in pick-up sticks, the removal of a single piece brought the whole edifice tumbling down. Quiet times followed, at least for eyes incapable of seeing the bustle of microscopic life. Until a pack of coyotes began to frequent the cave, and the cycle started over: it was like the previous time around but not – it never is – quite the same. The life cycle that turns on shit, on guano, on bountiful excrement: the unwitting gift of one living thing to another, enabling existence to go on. Shit as the link, the fundamental bond in the mosaic of organisms.

Discreet and persistent, clinging to its piece of rock on the very threshold of the light, the moss appeared to be one and the same over time. Hungry insects moved through its quilt, and spores that would later be scattered by the wind.

And there, in the farthest depths of the cave, blind and silent, lived the troglobites. A parallel world with no memory of sunlight. Those dwellers in underground tunnels and waters had grown accustomed to moving slowly and, after so long in the deep and the dark, had lost all colouring. Even when life on the surface changed, the troglobites remained unaffected. And later they vanished without ever having encountered the creatures that had seen the stars.

5

They arranged to meet in the cave because they came from enemy villages, always at war with one another. Nobody could remember how the enmity had begun, but it had existed for so long that neither village was prepared to give it up. The couple had thought about running away, but they were surrounded by dangerous places where they could be captured and sold as slaves. He had proposed hiding out in the mountains and living like hermits. She had asked him to give her a few days to sort out the turbulent rush of her thoughts.

And there they were at last, lying in the darkness of the cave. The girl laid her head on the boy's bare chest. The dripping of the stalactites echoed off the rock walls. The young couple could barely contain the feelings stampeding within them. There was something beautiful and poisonous in that suffering, she thought, as she caressed the boy's square chin, where just a few bristles had sprouted. She loved him, she was certain of that, but she was not cut out for the life of a fugitive. She had come to say goodbye. She would get married to someone else and lead the life that her people expected her to lead. But imagining the days to come made her feel so wretched that her heart rebelled. What if they did run away? It was easy to say now, with a full stomach and the time of the frosts a long way off . . .

The thing that tortured her most of all was that nobody knew they loved each other. In a few years they would die, and there would come a time when none of those who knew them by name and now walked the earth would be alive, and it would be as if what had sprung up between them had never existed at all. And this thought made her attachment to the boy more daring and more desperate.

I'll see you here in two weeks, she said defiantly, ready for whatever they had to face.

By the following week she was married to a man from her village.

Some years later, while out with her oldest daughter gathering herbs, she passed by the cave. She searched in her heart for a memory of the boy.

She was surprised to find that she could barely recall his features.

6

A stalactite is a series of drops in time. It forms as drop after drop of water seeps slowly from a crack in the roof of a cave. Each drop that hangs deposits a fine layer of calcite. Successive drops add one ring after another, and the water runs down inside the rings, gradually forming a tapered, pendent cylinder. Stalagmites grow upwards from the floor of a cave where water drips from stalactites. When a stalactite meets a stalagmite – in a dance that lasts tens of thousands of years – a column is formed. Until recently the ages of mineral formations could be calculated only if they were less than five hundred thousand years old, but it is now possible to date formations as old as eighty million years. So we now know that many stalactites and stalagmites made their first timid appearances in the time of the dinosaurs.

Caves have other kinds of mineral formations: some are shaped like curtains, or pearls, or delicate limestone helices; others resemble the canine teeth of dogs. One of the most spectacular caves lies beneath the Naica mine in Chihuahua: gypsum has formed translucid beams there, whole underground nests of colossal crystals.

The mine has been operating since 1794, but it was only in 2000 that these crystals the size of buildings were discovered by a pair of brothers who were digging a new tunnel. The heat is so intense it can only be borne for ten minutes without personal protective equipment, and crystal thieves have roasted underground. Within the crystals are archaic microorganisms that were trapped in bubbles of liquid fifty thousand years ago and have managed to remain in a dormant state like microscopic zombies. In 2017 those bacteria were reanimated in a laboratory. The scientists concluded that they were not closely related to any known microorganism.

7

The portal limned itself in the air and Onyx Müller materialised in the cave. Disconcerted, they looked around: this didn't seem to be the port where they were meant to disembark. They sent an urgent message to their fellow players, but the signal on their device was awash with static. Some interference had shunted them to an unindexed location in the deep web. Instead of a virtual replica of the Woodstock festival, 1969, the platform had delivered this dank scene. Onyx tried the back-to-base transmitters, but they were out of service. The recreation of the cave was pretty convincing, they had to admit. The sole of their left boot squashed an insect with long antennae. The bug went crunch and a viscous liquid like the goo in Bubbaloo gum spurted out.

Onyx Müller approached the mouth of the cave in search of a portal from which to re-establish contact. The light from outside was blinding: on crossing the threshold the scene would liquefy like melting plastic and the programme would return them to their colleagues – or so they expected. Instead they found themself in a dense forest of conifers, where birds were warbling. The landscape looked like a copy of the 3D poster in the old Café California, where the best chocolate-iced doughnuts of their childhood had been served. Something disturbed the tops of the pines: the rugged neck of a dinosaur. When its shadow fell on Onyx Müller, they looked up for the storm of pixels, but the wings of the pterosaur stood out sharply against the sky overhead.

8

His family had decided to emigrate, but he wanted to stay. He couldn't imagine living anywhere else; he was too old and, unlike his descendants, utterly incurious about interstellar travel.

Left on his own, he began to frequent the cave. He liked the golden moths that nested there and was also intrigued by the ancient paintings on the walls. No one really knew what sort of creatures had painted them or why they had disappeared, and no one apart from him had any desire to find out. It was a sign of decadence to look back at the past: his relatives were always founding new colonies, mutating and adapting. To them, his obsession with things from bygone times was obscene, and they made a great effort to keep it secret. So his decision to remain behind had come as a relief to them all.

In his last days he enjoyed scratching around in the debris that had built up on the floor of the cave, cleaning the various objects and putting them in order. He found the shell of an armadillo, an animal that had long been extinct, and a woman's fancy bracelet set with precious stones. His favourite thing was an intact Coca-Cola bottle, which he polished till it sparkled; when he blew on it through a tentacle, it made a music that reminded him of the wind demons in his birthplace.

Before dying he wanted to give birth one last time. He tucked some moth larvae into his abdominal fold and set off into the deepest passages of the cave to be devoured by the troglobites.

9

All that remained of the cave was a small hill, on which the violet bird alighted. The plain was covered with iridescent mushrooms puffing little clouds of spores up into the air. Moist, blue larvae wriggled in the earth. The bird dug out a big fat one with its long, speckled beak. It was hungry: with the rest of the flock, it had just returned from the warm lands. They had flown over meadows, volcanoes, petrified forests, mushroom plains and ancient sunken cities, arriving just in time for the larval season. In a couple of days, the grubs would sprout wings and antennae, turn poisonous and devour the mushrooms, but now was the ideal time to prey on them: they were in peak condition. The bird scratched at the ground and laid a golden egg. The caps of the mushrooms quivered in the breeze, which scattered the opalescent mist of spores. Soon a light shower fell over the plain.

Atomito

One day the Special Anti-Crime Force conducts a raid in the Low City's Chinatown, searching for goods stolen from luxury homes in a series of recent armed robberies. Along with guns, jewellery, drugs of all kinds and electrical appliances, the officers discover colonial artworks, looted decades ago from various rural churches and sold on the black market. There are silver chalices, carved wooden angels with arquebuses, paintings of Saint George and the Dragon, and altarpieces, all taken from old chapels on the altiplano to decorate the living rooms of the rich. The police also find pedigree dogs and fighting cocks from clandestine breeding farms. The operation dismantles the gang of thieves and returns the goods to their owners with ample media coverage, but the whole question of the trafficking in viceregal artworks is handled discreetly, given the involvement of eminent local families.

One of the restorers in charge of the recovered works detects an anomaly in a painting. It's an eighteenth-century picture showing the Virgin in the form of a mountain, which is how the indigenous painters managed to smuggle the worship of Pachamama into Christian iconography. The restorer notices that on the upper part of the canvas, the rays emanating from the Virgin – or rather, from the mountain – encounter another figure. It seems at first to be a rather complicated cloud, but closer examination reveals the faint silhouette of a child with a flowing, sky-blue cape. This is not a conventional figure or a common way of portraying angels, which leads the restorer to suspect that the painting is a forgery. But X-ray imaging confirms its authenticity.

What or whom could this figure represent, the restorer wonders. The son of an eighteenth-century aristocrat? Or some forgotten Andean deity?

There is a brief mention of this painting in the press, but it's soon buried by more important news.

※

Young people gather in a house in El Alto. To get there they have to avoid the police patrols in the streets. They have to go by foot, threading the stray dogs and burnt tyres, under the open eye of the icy night sky bristling with stars. Sometimes they're stopped and their backpacks are searched for sticks of dynamite or homemade bombs, although possessing or wearing a Wiphala is enough to trigger an interrogation.

The house they visit faces a patch of wasteland. It's an unplastered brick house with a half-built second storey and a gravity-defying design, like many of the dwellings in the area. The neighbours use the wasteland to dump their rubbish: carcasses of fridges and old stoves stand there like monoliths beneath the sky of the altiplano.

From the second storey of the house you can see the twinkling lights of the Power Plant and the shops a third of a mile away: a beautiful swarm of fireflies. By day you can also see the army tanks guarding the facilities, dragging themselves from one side of the perimeter to the other like listless caterpillars.

Kurmi Pérez is the name of the girl who receives the visitors, and she has been living on her own since her mother died a few weeks ago. Kurmi came home from university to find her mother dead on a chair in the kitchen, with her eyes open and a mug of maté in her rigid hand – she hadn't even tried to get to the hospital. From the coldness of that hand, Kurmi knew that her mother had been dead for several hours, and when she took it in hers, the cold jumped across into her body, got under her skin like a worm and crept up to settle in her brain. Since then, she's been dogged by an intermittent headache and can't get warm no matter how many of her thick, hand-knitted woollen jumpers she piles on.

The girl's heavy make-up accentuates rather than hides the rings under her eyes, making them look like two black holes. She hates her name, which means rainbow: so cheesy. When she opens the door to her friends, she always scans the vicinity, scared that they might have been followed by a drone. They go up to the second storey, where there's no furniture except for a small altar with a photo of her mother, surrounded by coca leaves, lit by electric candles of every colour. In the opposite corner is a Yamaha synthesiser that one of the boys got secondhand at the El Alto market. Kurmi rubs her cold hands; a skinny dog barks in the street. Someone pulls a bottle of Singani from a backpack, and the drinking begins.

※

Never Orkopata, better known as Orki, who used to work as a party DJ down in the Low City, had all his contracts cancelled when the disturbances began. Yoni delivers broaster chicken on a motorbike, wearing an orange helmet in the shape of a rooster's crest; his father died of cancer, and he's saving to pay back the money he borrowed to buy the coffin for the burial. Percéfone Mamani's brother, who was hit by a stray bullet in the protests against the Plant, is still in a coma; the doctors don't know if he will regain consciousness. Moko, the youngest of them all, dropped out of high school and works as a pajpaku on the dragon minibuses, selling magic crystals and rings that change colour according to the aura of the person wearing them. Kurmi had to give up her studies too so she could take over her mother's job knitting woollen dolls stuffed with polyester, but her fingers are clumsy, and she keeps dropping stitches; they've already sent back two of her orders.

Up there on the second storey, they laugh at sick jokes, get drunk, fight, cry, fall asleep clutching enormous plush tigers and wake up so numb with the cold they sometimes can't tell if they're dead or alive.

There are days when they see one of the curfew-enforcing drones veer about like a drunken bird, stop mid-air and drop into the street, out of juice, to the joy of the neighbourhood kids, who rush to strip it for sellable parts.

There are days when the police go into a neighbour's house, and they can hear shouts and the noise of things smashing.

There are days when they drink so much they forget to eat.

There are days when they're hungry but there's no money or food.

There are days when the city wakes wrapped in a fog so thick it's impossible to make out the shapes of things.

When the fog finally evaporates, sucked up by the winter sun, tanks can be seen proceeding in single file to the Plant for the changing of the guard.

❈

There's a lamp outside Kurmi's place, a stoic little streetlamp that throws a patch of greenish light on the pavement. The pole is covered with stickers that show the childish, smiling face of Atomito, the Plant's mascot, 'everybody's super friend', with his freckles, blue cape and white boots. The light also falls on the wall of the building opposite, where uneven lettering reads:

ELECTRICAL APPLIANCES REPAIRED

Lots of people used to turn up there with old TVs, burned-out irons, broken tablets and damaged microwaves to get them repaired and re-repaired, but since the technician got sick, the door of the workshop has remained shut, secured by a solid steel padlock.

The neighbourhood is named La Yareta after the huge fluorescent cushion plant that grows on the wasteland, from which the locals occasionally take cuttings to make a cough remedy. Kurmi's mother once told her that the plant grows a quarter of an inch per year at the most, so it would have taken more than twenty centuries for it to reach that size. The houses of La Yareta, on the other hand, sprang up in less than a decade, like a cluster of mushrooms stubbornly clinging to the trunk of a crooked tree, without council permission or any but the most rudimentary planning. Kurmi remembers how, as a girl, she would queue up with her mother to fill their buckets at the only public tap, very early in the morning, when the sun had just begun to rim the mountain peaks with silver. This was years before the people from the council came handing out flyers with the logo of the Plant. The officials promised to give the residents property titles and make La Yareta a model neighbourhood with all the basic services: water, sewage, electricity. Soon after that, they paved the roads, and construction began behind the wire fence.

Kurmi and her mother felt lucky to live near the Plant, although the tyres of the dragon minibus were soon thumping into the potholes that had opened all over the surface of the new road. Kurmi has never set foot in the Plant, but one of her neighbours in La Yareta – a woman who'd come from the same Aymara village, driven away by three years of drought – worked in one of the cafeterias. The woman spoke to them of gardens where roses bloomed all year round, employees in blue overalls operating the reactor's three towers, the convention centre with its marble floor shining like a licked lolly, the hotel for international visitors with its own cinema and the real-lawn tennis courts.

What nobody knew much about were the metal drums holding waste from the Plant, piling up in the warehouses. According to a rumour, this was no ordinary rubbish but a kind of material that had to be managed in a very particular way. Still, that was just one of the many legends about the place that were going around.

Kurmi's mother bought blue and white wool and knitted an Atomito doll, with which her daughter held long conversations before going to sleep. Atomito, the boy with the blue cape, took her by the hand, and off they flew to visit the Plant. There they played hide and seek – Atomito's childish laughter echoing in all the corridors – went sliding down the hotel's bannisters, followed the engineers into the towers, manipulated the control panels with their brightly coloured buttons, and when they got tired, they settled down with huge bottomless cups of Coca-Cola to watch cartoons in the cinema.

When the roads were paved and the streets were lit, lots of people suddenly wanted to move to La Yareta, and not just new arrivals from the country: moneylenders too, costume makers for the Virgen del Carmen parade, chicha vendors attracted by the boom, truck drivers, mattress salesmen, even a businessman who'd done so well importing Chinese textiles that he was able to build himself a cholet. Very few of these people took much notice of the protests against the construction underway beyond the patch of wasteland: the activists were saying that a plant like that should never have been located so near a city, and some superstitious people believed that a powerful wak'a dating back more than a thousand years was buried there and might awaken at any moment. Most people, however, agreed that the protestors were motivated by envy or pig-headedness.

The last time they talked, her neighbour showed Kurmi her security pass for the Plant: a biometric card with the slogan, 'I will return and I will be neutrons' in elegant, iridescent script beside an image of Túpac Katari. Things got complicated after that, and they lost touch, until one day Kurmi heard that her neighbour was very ill. By that stage, her mother was ill too, Atomito lay forgotten at the back of a wardrobe, and people were getting suspicious about the Plant.

❋

One electric, windy night, Percéfone turns up at the house on the wasteland with scratches all over her face. She has spent the afternoon arguing with the doctors attending to her brother in a hospital down in the Low City. Although she kept insisting that her brother was shot in the head on his way to his job at a hardware shop, the doctors reported him as a terrorist. The newspapers identified Percéfone's brother as a member of the lawless mob from El Alto that gathered with placards outside the Plant to protest against its operation. If he comes out of the coma one day, a police cell will be waiting for him.

When Percéfone was about to get into the dragon minibus to return to El Alto, three Low City otakus appeared on the corner, malevolent sneers on their faces, fingers stacked with expensive rings. The most obnoxious of the three yelled: 'Radioactive cunt!' Percéfone confronted them, jackknife in hand. The otakus jumped her; the blade went flying through the air like a ninja star, and fell through the grate of a drain. Percéfone had learned karate from Maestra Cusicanqui, who gives the women of El Alto martial arts classes in Aymara, in return for help in her vegetable garden. With a few karate moves, Percéfone was able to neutralise the delinquents, leaving them sprawled on the ground, to the astonishment of passersby. But in the course of the fight, she lost her purse as well as her knife, so she had to beg the driver of the last dragon minibus to let her ride back up for free before curfew began.

Moko laughs at the 'radioactive cunt', and Percéfone slaps him in the face. Tears she has struggled to hold back all day begin to shine on the girl's reddened cheeks. The others look away, deeply uncomfortable. They're all in a foul mood. The gusts of wind shaking the walls don't help. Nor does their hunger: shiny bones are all that's left of the quarter broaster that Yoni swiped from Bin Laden Chicken on his shift, collectively devoured a few hours ago.

To top it off, Yoni demands back the hundred pesos that Moko borrowed from him a while ago to buy a relic – a signed vinyl pressing of an album by Maroyu – and the argument sparks a diss battle in a mixture of Spanish and Aymara. Damn lunthata! Dumb q'ulu bastard! Dipshit! Jamarara! they yell at each other.

Kurmi curls up beside the little altar: her headache has become a magnetic fog, a cloud jumble gravid with electricity. Normally, a stern look from her would be enough to put them all in their places, but the mist of the migraine is blurring her vision. Each time Yoni and Moko shout, the voltage jumps in her brain, piercing it with dazzling, painful flashes. All she can do is pick up the ball of wool she left in the corner and try – fingers shaking, eyes shut tight, body rocking like a sea horse – to go on knitting the scarf that her mother left unfinished.

Propped in the window frame, facing away from the argument, Orki lights up a joint. Not so long ago he was DJ Orki: at the parties he played, it was cocktails in psychedelic colours on the house, and synthetic drugs to share with Sayuri, the most incredibly beautiful twistah ever to live in the high cities, with her lilac lock of hair, and that tiny star in her aquiline nose. Even if the parties start up again someday in El Alto, it will never be the same for Orki: at the beginning of the curfew Sayuri was found fast asleep with a bottle of pills beside her, and nobody could wake her up. Some say it was an accident; others claim she did it on purpose, harassed by a hikikomori in Pando, who was posting naked photos of her on social media.

Orki is sickened by the turn the night has taken – the night and the rest of his life. Scandalous, fat drops of rain are hammering at the roofs. The sky is sparking over the wasteland like a knife ground on a whetstone, and the moon is the narrowest silver slice peeping out between masses of electric cloud. Klepto! Shitty k'ewa! Lap'arara! Anu q'ara asshole! China jamp'atita! And *that*, it seems, is just too much for Yoni, who grabs the bottle of Singani and hurls it at Moko, who dodges. It shatters against the wall. The noise galvanises Kurmi's brain. The migraine building since her mother died blows out like a mushroom cloud, unleashing a psychic storm:

¡BASTA!

With his elbows resting on the windowsill, Orki sees the landscape lit by a discharge so massive it seems for a moment he's looking through a photographic negative. The lightning bolt hits one of the towers of the Plant and passes right through it, lighting it up from inside. The jagged ray writhes up and down the tower – a cable linking earth and sky – and lunges into the violet clouds like a luminous snake springing up from the ground.

Orki wants to call to the others, but not a word comes out of his mouth. A viscous light is bubbling out of the tower's base, spreading beyond the perimeter, engulfing the appliances dumped in the middle of the wasteland. The earth has cracked open and something long hidden is pouring out in all directions. Orki wants to close his eyes and obliterate that vision, but his eyelids have turned to stone. A second before the lights go out all over the city, he feels a spreading warmth in his groin.

❀

Hi! I'm Atomito, Everybody's Super Friend. Come with me and see how I live in the Túpac Katari Nuclear Research Plant. Look! We're coming to District C76 in the city of El Alto. This house here belongs to the fabulous Kurmi Pérez, but today I want to show you my little house in the reactor: it's a total blast! Let's have a look! This is the highest place in the world where a nuclear plant has ever been built. See how cute it is! This pretty building houses the Multipurpose Radiation Centre. Boxes of fruit, meat and other foods are processed here, using controlled radiation to eliminate pathogens and harmful bacteria. This is where I have a shower after I've been out! And this building is the Research Reactor. I don't actually have permission to enter, but I'm clever; when the engineers aren't looking, I sneak in and leave orange peels on the floor for them to slip on. Those barrels they're taking to the sheds? They're full of funny glowing stuff that's great to play with. Let's tip them over! Ha ha. I love a joke. Want to know my favourite trick? Disintegrating and escaping up through the chimney as vapour. That way no one can catch me! Don't worry, friends! All these structures are perfectly safe. Their design and operating conditions conform to standards set by the International Atomic Energy Agency. To prove it, I'm going to light this little match. Look!

❊

When Orki comes to, it's dark all around him, and the Plant's emergency siren is wailing like a muffled, surly car horn. The voices of the others explain: the lightning that hit the Plant has caused a power failure throughout El Alto. Yoni, Moko and Percéfone have made peace in the blackout. Their drunkenness, dispelled by fear, has given way to a tense lucidity. They make fun of Orki: after all that playing the tough guy with his drugs, one little rain shower and he falls apart.

Orki laughs too. He thinks the tremendous lightning flash must have made him hallucinate that light spurting up out of the earth, those luminous tentacles spreading in the night. But there's an inner uneasiness that he can't put to rest; he's ashamed to have wet his jeans in front of the others, and he feels strange... as if magnetised. Twitches pass through his body, his muscles conspire among themselves, the hairs on the back of his neck are standing up straight, and when he rubs his hands together, it generates a small but unmistakable bundle of electricity, which no one else seems to notice.

Moko tries to light a tallow candle that he found in one of the kitchen drawers, but the wind keeps blowing out his lighter's feeble flame. In its brief flash he glimpses a silhouette: Kurmi, knitting away in the darkness, placid and quiet. She hasn't said a word, and her contented calm seems odd to all her friends, especially after such an outburst. Still, it's better to see her like this.

Yoni goes over to the window, intrigued by the unusual activity beyond the perimeter fence: from the intersecting beams it looks like people are running around in the downpour with spotlights and torches. In the other direction, the city is still plunged in a darkness thicker than the mud of Choqueyapu. Percéfone peers over Yoni's shoulder at the shadow-flooded alleys. Yoni shudders; it isn't fear, he tells himself, it's just Percéfone's breath softly tickling him behind the ear.

❄

With the first ray of sunlight they are woken by a voice; it's the evangelical pastor who preaches through a hologram that wanders all over the city:

'We do not come from evolution!!! We are not related to monkeys!!! God created you in your mother's womb!!!'

The kids are dazed and sleepy, and it takes them a few minutes to realise that Orki is gone. After the power failed, while the others went back to drinking, he lay down beside the little altar and covered himself with a blanket to hide the wet patch. No one heard him leave. Yoni looks out the window. The sky has cleared; houses are reflected in the puddles all over the street; a sodden condor is resting on the dumped fridge by the path. There's a lot of activity behind the wire fence: men in helmets and overalls have climbed the towers and are trying to repair the damage caused by the storm. From a distance they look like tiny decorative figures on a candy fort, about to be flung off by a gust of wind.

By the light of day, the events of the previous hours blend into a turbid dream. But the news is circulating on their phones: overnight the terrorists of El Alto struck again, this time trying to blow up the Plant; the police announce further raids and new security measures until such time as the culprits are found.

'The fuck they talking about, terrorist bands?! It was the lightning,' says Moko, remembering.

The only one who doesn't seem worried is Kurmi: she announces with a mysterious smile that her migraine is gone and she feels like a smoke.

❊

Hours later, when Yoni is delivering orders for Bin Laden Chicken on his beaten-up Kawasaki, his mobile phone flashes repeatedly. Whenever he gets onto the bike and pulls on the helmet with its rooster crest, the city tilts like a 3D track in a video game, and the wheels lift an inch off the ground. With the help of his laser vision and razor-sharp reflexes, he dodges the dragon minibuses spitting fire as they pass, the drunks sprawled on the pavement and the street vendors hawking jelly with whipped cream, all the while racing the Ratuki cholas on their motorbikes, and losing the packs of furious street dogs that chase the scent of broaster chicken.

When he reaches his destination at the time specified by the app, and an arm emerges from the half-open door of a house or a flat to take the hot, fragrant order of Bin Laden Chicken, gold coins rain down from the sky and an announcement flashes before his eyes:

> MISSION ACCOMPLISHED
> YONI HAS UNLOCKED
> THE NEXT STAGE

If he manages to avoid all the obstacles put in his way by the chaos of the city and never run late, his boss – a bot by the name of Cornelio Artex – will drop him an end-of-year bonus, with which he's hoping to finish paying off his father's coffin and, if there's some left over, buy a bus ticket to Arica, so he can check out the sea. Which means he always has to keep an eye on his phone, never miss an order, and weave his way through the city at lightning speed.

While Yoni's waiting for the traffic lights to turn green (the zebras are doing handstands on the pedestrian crossing in front of him), he checks the orders coming in on the app. But other, more urgent, messages appear on top. It's Moko and Percéfone, independently sending him a video that's going around on social media, followed by exclamation marks.

!!

The video shows a young man in a trance walking through the alleys of the market, surrounded by mountains of tubers and bunches of parsley and huacataya. Although there's no music playing or any festivity going on, the young man is dancing. Except it's not so much a dance, thinks Yoni, as a series of weird convulsions, as if the cops were at him with a cattle prod. The vendors point at him and laugh. 'He's drunk,' says a chola. 'Hey, where's the party?' yells another, and tosses him a corn cob, which hits him on the head and knocks back the hood that was covering his face. His eyes are white, rolled back in their sockets, but Yoni can tell right away from the piercing in his eyebrow and the diamond tattoo on his neck that it's Orki.

'Orki is under a spell,' he says.

The lights turn green and a hysterical chorus of horns starts up behind his motorbike.

✺

Videos of the deranged dancer are going viral. On social media the kids are getting news from all over El Alto that Orki has been sighted, moving in that convulsive way. Some people throw dirty water at him from their windows. Some whistle. Others, tired of the curfew and the surveillance, clap and play cumbia chica to accompany his dance. Memes are made.

In the evening, Moko boards a crowded dragon minibus passing through La Ceja to hawk his new product: a bag of pumpkin seeds that he removed from his grandmother's kitchen:

Gooooooood afternoon to you all, ladies-gentlemen-girls-boys-artificial-intelligences, it's not my intention to interrupt or inconvenience you, quite the contrary; I'm here today to tell you about the latest marvel of science. Direct from the laboratories of Moscow to the homes of El Alto, I bring you the fruit of years of research by the world's most renowned genetic engineers: these pumpkin seeds endowed with special, amazing, fabulous properties! Don't let the simplicity of their appearance fool you, ladies-gentlemen-girls ... these are much more than ordinary seeds: they have been modified to adapt themselves to any soil, they have even been planted on Mars ...

A man wearing a T-shirt and cap bearing the logo of the local council looks up with interest. Moko, approaching to show him the seeds, glances out the window of the dragon minibus and sees Orki jerking along the pavement, followed by new dancers. One of them is the woman who threw the corn cob at him in the market; now she's doing a twisted jive with her eyes rolled back. The other is a very thin old man, jumping like a grasshopper. Moko cranes his neck to see where they're headed, but just then the council employee shows him a laminated card that says OFFICE FOR CONSUMER PROTECTION and asks to see his health department authorisation to sell seeds.

Moko yells Stop!, jumps off the dragon minibus and runs, pursued by the employee.

The vendors setting up on the pavement keep their distance from the strange procession, unsure what it's about. And the dancers keep making their way through the city, oblivious to the reactions provoked by their passage.

A few blocks from La Ceja, near the Cruz Papal, Yoni has stopped responding to the orders from Bin Laden Chicken and is trying to track down Orki, although he knows it won't be easy. Worried about what the police might do to his friend, he rides to the places where Orki has been filmed, but by the time he gets there, the group has always moved on. This is the real test: he has to be faster, he thinks, hitting the Kawasaki's throttle and running a string of red lights. By the end of the afternoon, there's a whole crowd dancing in the streets, to judge from the images captured by a drone hovering over the city. And what those images show is that the dancers are starting to head for the Plant.

❊

Kurmi takes a plastic chair out onto the patio and sits there knitting, facing the patch of wasteland: the yareta is a huge mass of green foam standing out against the lunar landscape. Two thousand years ago, she thinks, when it opened its first tiny rosette, other gods inhabited the earth; in another thousand or two thousand years, the yareta plant will still be alive. What will be left of this world two thousand years from now? she wonders.

'The mountains,' her mother's voice replies, clear as a bell. 'Would you like me to tell you the story of how the mountains walk? You liked to hear it when you were little.'

Kurmi looks up at the Cordillera: sometimes it seems to be a mirage produced by the sun on the altiplano.

'Once there was a girl who went out to tend a flock of llamas and, gazing at the mountain to her left, fell asleep on a rock. The girl didn't know, but the rock on which she had lain down was a very ancient and powerful wak'a. The wak'a made the girl fall into a deep sleep, which lasted for hundreds of years. When she woke up, the llamas had been replaced by tall buildings, and now the mountain was on her right. Don't just see how things look to you, see how they look to the yareta,' says her mother. 'Only then will you understand how the mountain walks.'

Kurmi smiles: she has heard the story dozens of times, and could hear it dozens more. Her fingers are plying the knitting needles, working the wool, but the movements are not hers – they belong to her mother. Her mother is happy to get back to her knitting. And

Kurmi is not about to let her go away. The scarf is already nine feet long; it's becoming unwieldy, impossible to wear.

'What did you do with Atomito, Kurmi? It's time to knit you a new doll.'

They haven't stopped talking since the lightning strike. A comet hummingbird with an iridescent red tail and a metallic green breast whirs past on its way to the other end of the empire. Beyond the blurry line of the perimeter, the reactor's chimney belches voluminous white fumes. The girl is watching as she knits: that's not steam coming out of the mouth of the reactor. All the engineers in the country couldn't repair the damage done. It's something older issuing from the open heart of the earth. It isn't steam, she repeats. In Kurmi's head, her mother bursts out laughing. And the air brings the echo of the laughter of a child, made from the stuff of dreams.

'It's souls,' she says to her mother.

※

DJ Orki is dancing with Sayuri under the strobe lights of a disco that stretches away in every direction; wherever you look, salons and sounds open up, and dancers pass with drinks in their hands, masked as jukumari bears, kusillos, even dinosaurs.

'You came back,' says Orki.

The girl smiles: behind the glitter lipstick her teeth are a dazzling white. And now it's as if Sayuri had never gone away. The desire passing between them creates a magnetic field strong enough to revive the hidden, buried city. Maybe Orki thinks the crowd all around him is made up of guests at that party without a beginning or an end; maybe he's unaware that they are creating the party as they go, and that it's heading for the Plant.

In the Low City, fear lights up like red alarm-bell icons. The TV channels warn of violent, insurrectionary mobs threatening the Plant, and police patrol cars race up to El Alto.

Yoni's motorbike whizzes between the dragon minibuses stuck in a jam at La Ceja. Little does he know that for all his haste he is destined never to arrive; in less than a minute, at the corner up ahead, an ambulance will smash into him, and the last thing he will see as he flies through the air – still wearing the rooster-crest helmet – will be a glittering shower of gold coins.

In the hospital, Percéfone's brother has just opened his eyes to the light pouring in through the window. The world is making itself anew, as if he had just been born.

Surrounded by ferns and cacti in his Low City

studio, the restorer at work on the eighteenth-century painting has noticed how the figure of the child above the Virgin mountain is growing clearer and clearer. He raises a hand to his mouth, incredulous, staggered by his new discovery.

Moko stops to catch his breath on the bridge in La Ceja; he has managed to shake off his pursuer, and the magic pumpkin seeds are safe in his pocket. But he has lost sight of Orki and the procession. He looks up at the storm cloud darkening the horizon, about to throw its shadow over the Low City. But right away he sees his mistake: that stain on the sky is not a cloud. He hears an echo of laughter, childish laughter from on high. The mass obliterating the sun has the form of a child wearing white boots and a flowing cape: it's Atomito coming up over the mountain.

Look!

The Debt

I'm accompanying my aunt to recover a debt in the village where she was born. The driver leads us through the train cemetery to his motorbike: his eagle-shaped belt buckle and the toe caps of his leather boots sparkle in the sun. The bike tears along over the paving stones and the melting tar. Each jolt shakes my belly, which makes me anxious; I have to be more careful from now on.

We stop for lunch at a shack with a view over the muddy river; we're the only customers. It's hot, and the blades of the single fan that hangs from the jatata-thatched roof groan with each half-hearted rotation. On the riverbank people have gathered around the body of a drowned man. A young guy who went fishing three days ago when the river was high because of the rains and didn't come back, says the woman who owns the restaurant, coming to the table with a big steaming pan.

I can't help associating the drowned man with what the woman has served up: another fruit of the river, tumbling around in my mouth, with its curious rubbery texture and taste of boiled chicken. My aunt notices my disgust and gives me a stern look. I finally manage to swallow without gagging, but the mouthful keeps rising back up my throat.

The owner of the restaurant is a chatterbox; her dyed hair is done up in a messy bun, loosely held in place by a chopstick. She wants to know what has brought us to this place. My aunt lies: we're on holiday, staying at the hotel La Eslava for a couple of weeks, she says. A pity the hotel's so run down, says the owner of the restaurant, but not many people come here any more. Then my aunt goes on to say that we've reserved a cabin on the *Reina de Enín*, for a cruise on the Mamoré River, over several days, she stresses.

In fact, we have barely enough money for the trip, and we're staying with an old acquaintance of my aunt – an elderly seamstress to whom we are very distantly related – until the debt is paid. I would like to tell my aunt what's wrong: the bumpy ride on the motorbike made me feel nauseous, and I think I might need to lie down. The body of the drowned man stretched out on the riverbank isn't helping either, although someone has finally fetched a sheet to cover him. But I say nothing. Before we came, my aunt said: These things have to be done in a certain way. Above all, don't attract attention. Whatever you do, don't attract any attention.

The woman asks what we thought of the meal and points out that her place is one of the few in the entire Amazon where that dish is served. She explains how it's prepared: you squeeze lemon juice onto the fresh meat and sprinkle it with parsley. The member has to be cut off with a special machete; after a while it grows back. And then the cycle is repeated, mutilating the same part of the animal while sparing its life. Great skill is required so as not to cut off too much flesh and cause a fatal loss of blood, the woman explains. There are careless cooks who accidentally go too far, and others who do it on purpose, because the dying animal gives off a very special odour. When the member grows back, it's always slightly darker and tougher than it was at first, which is why some clients are willing to pay through the nose for the first cut.

My aunt asks for the bill, and the owner of the restaurant goes back into the kitchen. The blood rushes to my head; my temples are burning unbearably. My aunt becomes very attentive and worried: Is there something wrong? It's nothing, I say. I've been on the verge of telling her so many times, but I'm scared of provoking an outburst of anger or tears. Especially now that we're here to sort out this debt that's eating her up. Sometimes I think she knows but has decided not to let on – she's an old hand at games of deceit and duplicity. Maybe I'm not protecting her from shame by hiding the news but secretly savouring my triumph: my pregnancy underlines her barrenness. I feel my condition is obvious, but according to a friend it depends on the angle of vision, the perspective, the sort of clothes you're wearing.

The owner of the restaurant puts her head around the kitchen door. I can't contain the upheaval in my stomach any longer; I open my mouth to retch, and what comes rushing out of me is the river's dark, furious, unstoppable surge.

Many years ago we used to have relatives here, my aunt says, but now there's no one left. They all moved away. This was the first place in the region to have a cinema. Our ancestors built a theatre in the middle of the jungle, and opera singers came from Europe. There were parties, guests arriving by steamboat, champagne toasts. The men set out from time to time to find new Indians for the rubber plantations – the jungle fevers made short work of them. Great-great-grandmother Felicia had the Hotel La Eslava built to provide accommodation for the foreigners who came from all over the world; a teardrop chandelier was brought from France for the salon. We lost it all, my aunt says, but never forget that we're not common; we come from a family with a good name.

Nothing here seems to have any life in it: to get to where the seamstress lives we go through an abandoned garden, scattered with blackened statues and half choked with weeds. The air smells of rotten eggs and sour, fermented broth.

The only thing binding us to this village is the debt we have come to recover.

The seamstress lives in an old house made up of several rooms in a row giving onto a verandah where hammocks are slung. She occupies one room and rents the others to a schoolteacher, a council employee and the family of a washerwoman. My aunt and I stay in the room at the end, where the tenants pile all the useless junk they can't bring themselves to throw away. A filthy little broom cupboard, says my aunt, inspecting the damp-stained sheets on the bed that we will be sharing.

The seamstress and my aunt greet each other with elaborate shows of affection, surprisingly, since they haven't seen each other in thirty years.

'You've come at last,' says the seamstress.

'While there's still something left,' says my aunt.

'Soon we'll be gone, too.'

The seamstress looks at me with an icy curiosity. Her hands stroke my face.

'Doesn't look like you, this daughter of yours,' she says.

'She's not mine,' my aunt replies.

'She's not my mother,' I confirm.

The seamstress lets her eyes linger on me for a long moment. I must have gone pale. But I'm enjoying the possibility that she might notice before my aunt does.

'Lunch made her feel queasy,' explains my aunt. 'Such delicate stomachs, young people these days.'

The three of us walk along the verandah, pushing through the suffocating heat. The seamstress points to the ruined eaves, beams and straw poking out over the red bricks.

'This place is termite-ridden,' my aunt whispers. 'Someday soon the whole thing will fall down.'

My aunt took charge of my upbringing and education but she never let me call her Mother. I used to lie to my school friends: She's my mother, I said. I didn't want to be the only foster child, the one who'd been taken in. They came back at me, surprised: But she's white. And I had to explain: It's because my father was dark. To correct that early tendency to lie, my aunt resorted to the cane.

I never knew my mother but I often dream of her. My aunt has kept some photos: a very tall woman with sad eyes and wild brows. The dreams are always anxious: I always see her from behind, walking ahead of me, and when I'm about to catch up with her, she turns a corner and disintegrates as if she were made of sand. My aunt says she cleared off years ago, following a foreigner, but friends I've shown the photos to are sure they've seen her somewhere, in a bus heading for the border, in a bank queue or sitting in a dentist's waiting room. Every so often I re-examine the photos to see if a trace of my mother lives on in any of my expressions. My aunt says it's better not to take after her in any way: Why do you want to be like her, when she never came back for you in all these years?

I'd like my daughter to inherit my mother's features, so I can see them in that new flesh and blood. That way at last I'll have something that's mine, something my aunt can't take away.

At night I can't get to sleep because of the murmuring of the termites. The house is full of hungry jaws chewing their way through the walls, destroying the foundations. They're everywhere: behind the stacks of old magazines, under the shelf piled with headless dolls, between the sacks of rice in the pantry. My aunt dreams restlessly beside me: tossing and turning, riddled with shivers, whispering as if to a lover. I'm scared that if I shut my eyes the roof will fall in on us, so I stay awake until dawn.

The seamstress is waiting for us at breakfast with tea and empanadas. She says that our visit has made her notice the terrible state of the house, so she has called the exterminator to take care of the termites.

'I have to run some errands, but I'll be back before noon,' she says, excusing herself.

'She's leaving me to pay the bill, the stingy old bag,' says my aunt, who looks a little tired but otherwise untroubled by the goings-on last night.

The exterminator arrives mid-morning carrying a knapsack with a narrow white hose hanging from the bottom. My aunt doesn't like people who work with poison – she says it's a cowardly way of killing – so when the man turns up, she refuses to greet him and sends me out to show him around. I shouldn't be anywhere near poison, being pregnant, but I have no choice. He examines the furniture and sprays his product into the dubious corners. Soon the house will be an insect cemetery.

'You and your mum will be able to sleep easy,' says the man.

I don't correct him. The exterminator says he's going to check for nests outside the house: termites often have underground colonies far from the places where their activity is detected. The man points out a mound of earth in the garden, among the bougainvillea. That must be the queen's nest, he says. I imagine her seated on a throne, planning her revenge, and I start to feel the dizziness again, the shooting pains in my head. I can't put off telling my aunt any longer; I have to give her time to get used to the idea. The man grabs a spade and plunges it into the earth: the wound reveals an architecture of winding but abandoned tunnels. The soldiers have raised the alarm and the whole court has fled.

The man digs deeper, excavating secret passageways. Suddenly the spade hits a hard surface. He bends down and pulls something out of the earth, a root clasped around something else. He has to struggle to wrench that object free: it's a rag doll with human hair, darkened by the dirt. He hands it to me, and I shake off the earth to clean up the doll a bit, curious to see its face. Now the man is busy tugging at the root, which is long and tough. A very deep tunnel opens up in the ground.

The doll has no face; its head is all one mop of long, messy hair falling forwards and backwards. It looks the same whichever way I turn it. I drop the doll in shock and see it falling into that bottomless hole, the hair spread out in all directions: a flying spider.

'Why didn't you get married?' I hear the seamstress say. 'You were a prize; there were plenty after you.'

They're rocking back and forth in the hammock, with rhythmic, synchronised movements. With their backs to the night like that, they look almost a hundred, about to fall apart.

'Oh, for the love of God, don't be ridiculous!' says my aunt.

Sometimes my aunt talks to herself:

The last man of our line is still here; he took refuge in the jungle. They say he has a boat and fishes for a living. But no one in the town has seen him for many years. The only news we have of him is from the gold traffickers and Indians who live on the other side of the river. He was very handsome, like the first of our ancestors to come to this land. Great-grandmother wanted him to have whatever was left after the auction. It was all to go to him and nothing, not a cent, to the daughters, to ensure that the name would live on proudly, as in the glory days when the estate was intact. All to him, although ever since adolescence he'd been a hopeless drunk and a troublemaker. The first time he killed a man, he was still a minor. He used to sleep in a hammock, clasping a revolver to his chest, fanned by three Cambas. A beast off the leash, a womaniser. In his old age he seems to have found some kind of peace. Great-grandmother Hortensia called for him when she was dying. He has to hand over the title deeds. If he wants to live like a wild animal, fine by me. But he has to think of his family, those who are left.

It's Sunday. I go with my aunt to what the locals call the market: three blocks shaded by dirty tarpaulins, where measly goods are sold at higher prices than in the city. A Yaminahua boy comes up and tries to sell me a parrot chick, still featherless.

I see her walking through a group of people, taller than all of the men. I recognise her at once, as if she were emitting a vibration that only I can pick up. I know instinctively that she's my mother and that I'm not dreaming. I know because there's a scent of shallots and cracklings in the air, and in my dreams there are never any smells. My aunt is haggling over the price of a fake designer handbag and doesn't notice when I slip away.

I follow the woman, guided by that head held high, standing out above the others. A shaved-ice vendor runs over my foot with his cart, and some jerk sees his chance and grabs my ass, never mind my condition. I strike out blindly and hit a woman, who insults me. This time I'm not going to let my mother get to the corner and disappear. I don't dare call out her name or Mother, so I keep yelling Excuse me! Excuse me!

My mother is wearing a long dress, and her hair – loose, black, dishevelled – hangs down to her waist. She stops in the middle of the street, waiting for me, within reach. Excuse me, I say, and grip her firmly by the arm, determined not to let her go. Her arm is soft, but not with the springy softness of flesh; it gives like a sack of rice. She turns towards me but I can't see her face: it's covered by hair, like the rest of her head. I push her, spin her around, but it's impossible to tell which side is the front and which the back—

I wake up with a cry stuck in my throat.

'There's something you need to know.'

While my aunt is napping under the mosquito net, the seamstress takes me to her room. Each piece of furniture is adorned with a cover or a doily of her own confection.

'One of the workers from the huts got her pregnant and she ran away,' says the seamstress, hunched like a spider clinging to the wall, about to drop onto its prey. 'Whatever she tells you, she's your mother. That woman in the photos is just some stranger. She bought a bunch of old photos in a junk shop to make up a story for you to believe in. But it's better if you know where you come from.'

It all started coming undone when he said to me: It must have fallen under the bed.

I kneeled down and put my cheek on the cold tile floor; the television screen was giving off a snowy glow. I had just come out with what I'd been keeping bottled up inside: I'm sure it's going to be a girl.

I said it almost without thinking, and he stared back at me in silence, baffled. Then he thought aloud: It's not possible. The doctor said it was an ectopic pregnancy; you just had a curettage.

I shouted: What do you know!

I ran to the bathroom and shut myself in. He yelled through the door: You know I'm here for you.

We made it up, for a while at least. He even suggested some names. I didn't like any of them; they reminded me of flowers and pictures of crowned nuns. I wanted to give the girl my mother's name. To put off the moment of his departure, I stubbornly went on searching for the fallen buckle.

Did you find it? His voice was faint, as if he were retreating by leaps and bounds.

Under the bed it was raining; the light was very beautiful and very strange.

When I stood up he was gone.

I haven't heard from him since.

I'm tired, but my aunt doesn't want to stop: We're nearly there, she says, her voice rising over the hum of the bugs. The jungle scratches at our knees; we trip over roots as thick as arms. The hut on the riverbank swims into view, a floating mirage. A very old man with long, white hair is sitting in the doorway. He rests his pipe on his thin, tanned legs.

My aunt waves to him.

The old man reaches out to the side; the sun glints off the metal of the shotgun.

I hold my breath, and that's when the contractions begin.

Chaco

My grandfather used to say that every word has its guardian and the right word makes the earth shake. The word is a bolt of lightning, a tiger, a gale, the old man would say, staring at me angrily as he helped himself to the corner-shop alcohol, but woe betide anyone who uses words without due care. Do you know what happens to liars? he would ask. I'd try to ignore my grandfather by looking out the window at the vultures circling in the filthy sky over the town. Or I'd turn up the volume on his TV. Interference made the picture an explosion of tiny dots. Sometimes that was all we could see on TV: tiny dots. He'd keep on at me, my skeletal grandfather, brandishing his stick: Do you know what happens to people who lie? Words desert them, and once a man is empty, anyone can kill him.

He'd spend all day in his chair, drinking and arguing with his own drunkenness. At night, Mama and I would pick him up and drag him to his room; by then he was always so far gone he didn't know who we were. As a young man he'd been a violinist, and people from all over El Chaco would seek him out to play at parties, but the man I knew was housebound, unsociable, constantly whispering things to the liquor. Shut up, shut up, shut up, he'd tell the bottle fearfully, as if there were voices tempting him from within the glass. Other voices murmured in the tongue of the Indians. What's Grandpa saying, I asked Mama, as she went around the house putting down rat poison in the corners. L-l-leave G-g-g-randpa in peace, she said. C-c-curiosity is the D-d-d-devil's l-l-lure.

But one day El Colla Vargas said in front of everyone that when Grandpa was young he'd worked with the government people who drove the Matacos off their land. A peccary hunter had struck oil there when digging a hole to bury his dog, which had been bitten by a viper. The men from the government came with their guns, hunted the Matacos, burned down their houses and set up the Viper Oil Plant. Thanks to that oil field, a motorway was built, running along one side of the town. According to Vargas, a bunch of smart alecs had taken advantage of the eviction to rape Mataca women. Some of those women were blonde and blue-eyed, daughters of Swedish missionaries; they were prettier than ours, he said, those savages. My grandfather was never paid the money they'd promised him for getting rid of the Matacos, money he needed to settle a debt. He lost everything, went bad, became a drunk. That's what they say.

Nothing much ever happened in the town. Toxic clouds from the cement works fattened overhead. At dusk they shone with all the colours of the rainbow. If you didn't have a skin disease, you had a lung disease. Mama had asthma and took an inhaler with her everywhere. Foxes howled on the other side of the motorway. That's how the town got its name: Aguarajasë, Where the foxes howl. Every year the river got angry and rose up seething with mosquitoes. The world was far, far away. A man selling Tramontina kitchenware had got my mother pregnant when he was passing through, and no one ever heard of him again. Eighteen years later people were still talking about how, when the salesman was in town, the

Stammerer spoke without stumbling once, she was so in love.

One day, on the way home from school, I came across a Mataco lying on the side of the road. The guy was always drunk and harried by flies. He was tall and solidly built. The loincloth barely covered his balls. Dirty, degenerate Indian, people said. The truck drivers swerved to avoid him and honked their horns, but nothing could interrupt the Mataco's dream. What was he dreaming of? Why wasn't he with his people? I envied him. I wanted to get his attention, but to be what he was, he didn't need me. One day I picked up a big stone and threw it at him with all my strength from the other side of the motorway. It came down right on his skull. Crack! The Mataco didn't move but a red rivulet began to wind over the tarmac. The south wind was blowing so hard! It had been like that for days. It was full of the sound of alligator ticks. We listened anxiously in the dark. I didn't tell anyone what had happened. The next day two policemen took the Mataco away in a black bag. They didn't ask many questions; he was just an Indian. No one came to claim his body. I watched them cracking jokes as they threw the bag onto the back of the truck. I picked up the stone stained with the Mataco's blood, took it home and put it at the back of a drawer, behind my underpants.

Not long after that, the voice of the Mataco got into my head. Mostly he sang. He had no idea what had happened to him and moaned in that grief-stricken, swampy sort of voice they have. Ayayay, he sang. I dreamed his dreams: mobs of peccaries fleeing through the forest; the hot wound of a brocket deer struck by an arrow; vapours rising from the earth to become a part of the sky. Ayayay ... The Mataco's heart was a red fog. Who are you? What do you want? Why have you settled in me? I asked him. I am the Ayayay, the Avenger, He who Gives and Takes Away, the Kill Kill, the Rage that Explodes, said the Mataco, and he asked in turn: Who are you? There's no more you and me, I said. From now on our wills are one.

I was ecstatic, I couldn't believe my luck. I became very talkative. I'd open my mouth and before I knew it I was off, no going back: the Mataco's stories and mine got all mixed up. Doña María, the faggot says your father was swallowed by a whirlpool in the forest. Don Arsenio, according to your grandson, you skinned a jaguar and ate its heart raw. Is that true? Mama did the only thing she knew how to do: cry. Grandpa said I had the leprosy of falsehood and hit me so hard the stick broke in his hands. I had to go to school with bruises on my arms and legs, and put up with the stares of my classmates. Stares brimming with laughter. There goes the jaguar killer, said the stares, beaten up by the old drunk. I saw red everywhere, I saw everything burning with rage. The Mataco read my heart: Wait, don't rush, I'll tell you when your time comes.

Then the bikers rolled in. Everyone went to see because a cock fight had been set up for them, and Don Clemente had promised to bring out two of his champions. D-do you want to go? asked Mama. I didn't want to; the heat had given me a bad headache. As soon as Mama was gone, the Mataco started raising the red fog. The alligator ticks whistled inside me. The headache was blurring my vision. I went to the kitchen to get a glass of water. Shut up, shut up, shut up, the old man was saying to the bottle. The urine stain spreading like a spiderweb on his pants. He lifted his head and sat there looking into my eyes. Get out of here, you lazy, lying fag, he said. With the glass of water in my hand, I held his gaze. The old man defiant in his drunkenness. You're like sugar cane, empty inside, God knows what seed you sprang from, he said. And he spat on the floor with contempt. My blood ran riot, my veins were full of fire ants. The Mataco started jumping inside me. What are you waiting for? Don't you want your revenge, child of a red viper? Are you going to let the old drunk treat you like that? Is your blood as cold as a toad's? I went to get the stone. I came up behind Grandpa's chair and hit him hard on the side of the head, just once. He fell down. He panted hoarsely, life rushing out through his mouth. I stood there watching, surprised: so old and still clinging to this world?

Mama came back later and found him on the floor, drowning in his vomit. He had a fall when he was drunk, that's what people said in town. It took him days to die; he finally kicked the bucket on the seventh. I saw the soul come out of his body like a wisp of white smoke then float up and away. We sold the house to pay the hospital bill and moved into a room behind the shop at El Colla Vargas's place. That was all we could afford. His wife wasn't happy about it and greeted us grumpily. I heard her arguing with her husband: The Stammerer's kid is weird. Why did you let them come here? Unless there's something between you and that woman? Then she burst into tears. But she wouldn't have been jealous if she could have seen Mama as I saw her every night, with her tits hanging down to her waist under the nightie. Mama and I slept in the same bed. As soon as we got in, she'd turn her back to me and start praying herself to sleep. I'd stay awake, playing with the stone, which throbbed in my hands, and listening to the murmur of the other me: The cold came to the forest, the river ran dry in its bed. Ayayay. The frog jumped on the branch, the viper bit it in the head. The girl who went to fetch water, later she turned up dead. Ayayay. The young man who went out hunting, he turned up later, dead. Ayayay. The old man went home, they found him dead. Ayayay. The woman who danced with another man: dead. Ayayay. The man with the monkey laugh, him too: dead. Ayayay. And the woman with the pointy chin, too: dead. Ayayay. Nobody came forwards to take the corpses away. Ayayay. They started going bad among the bushes where they lay. Ayayay. The souls of the departed came back to cry, came back to stay. Ayayay. She said: Will we be left among spirits when the living have all gone away? And the next day she was gone herself. Ayayay. Son of a venomous spider, for you the wind is beginning to turn. This is the start of a new cycle, the sky is opening, watch out. Ayayay.

Sometimes Mama would stare at me as if she was about to say something. One day she announced that she was going to live on the other side of the river with an aunt who had lost her husband; I was free to do what I liked.

When are you going? I asked her.

R-r-right aw-w-way, she said. Her upper lip was trembling. She took a puff from the inhaler, the way she did when she was nervous. For the first time I knew how it felt to be feared; I liked it.

Wh-wh-wh-what is th-th-that st-stone you're always h-h-holding?

I picked it up off the road.

Wh-wh-what were you d-d-doing the d-d-day G-g-gr-grandpa fell?

Watching TV, I said.

She kept at me: You d-d-d-didn't h-h-hear anything?

The volume was way up, I replied.

The Stammerer pressed her lips together and, with a single look, disowned me:

I c-c-can't st-st-stand this anym-m-more, she said and retreated to the little room, slamming the door behind her.

I went for a walk. When I came back, the Stammerer had gone, taking all her things. What do we do now? I went out and looked at the motorway. Don't think twice, don't say goodbye, don't look back. Someone will stop and give you a lift. I went back in, put the stone and two changes of clothing in my backpack and left town without saying goodbye to Vargas or his wife. The clouds were floating high, loaded with poison. Within five minutes a truck stopped: a tanker taking fuel to Santa Cruz. The driver was on his own and happy to let me climb aboard. I didn't turn back for a last look at the town. We chewed coca leaves along the way and listened to a Guaraní radio station on and off. We saw miles of burned trees scratching at the sky. We saw a sloth with a burned back dragging itself along the motorway. We saw a sign that said Christ Is Coming and further on another one that said Bread and Gas Here.

The driver was one of those guys who's old enough to have a family somewhere but not too old to be up for a bit of action. He pulled over suddenly, parked the truck under some trees, tilted the seat back as far as it went, and unzipped his fly.

Go ahead, buddy, he said.

At first I was put off by the smell of urine and old man. But after a while I got a hard-on too. The dirty creep panted and jerked me off while I was blowing him. We came almost at the same time. He did up his fly, took a Casino from behind his ear, and smoked it, handing it over from time to time, but without looking me in the eye.

Case you're wondering, he said, the faggot's the one who sucks, OK?

He was cheerful, satisfied, pleased with himself. Do I kill him? If you kill the road man, you won't get to where they're waiting for you. Or is the white man kin to the scorpion that turns its sting back on itself? Ayayay. How about you shut up, smart-ass Indian. I'm so sick of your Ayayay. With the rattling of the truck and the wind buffeting the windows, I fell asleep and dreamed I was dying and a boy as beautiful as the sun was waiting for me on the far side of death. I cut out my tongue to give to him and was mute as I handed it over, but my heart called him by the name My Saviour. I woke up to the shudder of the engine shutting down.

We're going to stop here for a while, said the driver. It was a house in the middle of nowhere, its smashed-out windows covered with cardboard. A dark woman stood in the door frame smoking, sculpted in that pose. She was old, she must have been about twenty-eight. The wind was kicking up dust devils around her, whisking them away into the air. The driver handed her a bag of groceries, which she took without saying thank you. Two children were playing bottle-cap football on the kitchen floor. Neither looked up when we came in. The woman started brewing maté while the driver sat himself down on one of the plastic chairs. They didn't say a word and barely exchanged a glance, but each was alert to the movements of the other.

I could feel it in the air so I went for a walk along the path behind the house. The forest grew dense with caracoré cacti, covered with those fruit the blackbirds fly down to peck. In a clearing, a hot spring bubbled up like soup. The sun was shining in my face, and at first I was blinded by the glare off the surface of the water and the rising steam. Then I saw it. The octopus was lying on a rock. Its tentacles were writhing: fat pink boa constrictors with suckers the size of billiard balls. They were wrapped around a trembling fox cub, too scared to even try to escape. The creature looked like a huge lump of jelly melting in the sun. The place stank of fish, of women. When the octopus sensed me approaching from the bank, it curled up its arms like a fat lady hitching up her skirts to cross a river. Warily, quickly, it dragged itself down to the water's edge, leaving its prey behind. With a smack, the last tentacle disappeared; hot bubbles rose to the surface and burst. The little fox sprang away into the forest, free again, and soon all was still, as if the creature had never been there. Transparent fish, the kind with guts you can see, were feeding near the bank. But the giant creature must have been sleeping or waiting down in the depths. The murmur began to get louder in my head. The river turned to poison, the fish turned belly up and died. Hunger was great, hunger was long, and food in short supply. They sent three men out hunting, none of them came back alive. It was a dog that found their bones, picked all clean and white. Ayayay. Who gets to eat around here? the caracara cried. The forest laughed to itself, the light went out of the sky. The mother looked at a son she could no longer recognise. Where did the souls go when the earth split open, gaping wide? Ayayay. I listened to us and threw stones into the pool until I got bored.

When we got back to the house, the driver and the

woman had shut themselves in the bedroom. Their moans came in cascades. The children were still playing on the floor, paying no attention to the noise. The younger one was clumsy and had a head like a balloon, twice as big as normal. It was funny that we hadn't noticed right away: the boy had Down's syndrome. His mouth was hanging open and he kept dropping the bottle caps. His big head was nodding at us; it was like an invitation. We took the stone out of our pack and weighed it in both hands. The stone was throbbing, it was alive. Ayayay. The wind was galloping outside, making the timbers creak. With a jaguar's tread, we approached the boy and calculated how much force we'd have to use to waste him. His brother looked up and met our gaze; a spark flew between us. The kid understood right away, he was watching us curiously. We held that balance for a second. Then the door of the room opened and the driver appeared, wiping the sweat off his face with the hem of his shirt.

Time to go, buddy, he said.

We went back to the truck. Being interrupted like that put us in a bad mood. Our blood was up and it wouldn't settle down again. We didn't feel like talking. Luckily, now that he'd shot his load, the old creep had lost all interest in us and was concentrating on the road. We weren't about to give up. Do I kill him? Didn't I tell you no? Weren't you the Avenger, the Kill Kill? What are you talking about, brainless white man, born of the race that doesn't wait? Your heart is like the ant that sees nothing; all it can do is bite. I'm getting impatient, where's my task? When you have eyes to see, you'll see it for yourself.

We got to Santa Cruz as night was falling. The driver dropped us off at a set of lights and said if we kept walking we'd get to the plaza. So there we were, on our own, standing in the middle of the traffic, with cars coming and going in all directions. We didn't have a peso, or know where to spend the night. But we were our own boss. We let the rush of the crowd sweep us along, we let the racket of the street daze us; we carried a stone with us and our voice. The buildings rose up in every direction, and the city shone as if freshly polished.

That was when we heard the screech of brakes. The tyres of the car skidded over the tarmac and we flew up into the sky. All the air was knocked out of our lungs, the spirit came away from the body. A woman's scream reached us, bouncing off something. Before we fell our soul floated over the cars. A dove stared at us in surprise; we saw the people behind the windows of one of those tall buildings. And as we plunged, our eyes met the eyes of the driver: the most beautiful boy we'd seen in all the days of our life. He stared at us with his mouth hanging open, sheer amazement dancing in his eyes. It's the Beautiful One, from your dreams. My Saviour, we thought, recognising him, here is our tongue, we give it to you, our voice is yours. One last sound, and we embraced the darkness.

The Greenest Eyes

She spent her tenth birthday in her mother's village. Every holiday they went back to that place in the jungle where there were no cars, just motorbikes going round and round the plaza, and huge insects that kept frying themselves on the streetlamps. Her father bought mara wood there and took it to the city to make varnished furniture. As time went by, there were more timber cutters in the jungle, and fewer mara trees, and more varnished furniture with carved swans' heads in the fancy houses. Ofelia liked the village because she was allowed to play with the neighbourhood children until after midnight. Also, most of them rode motorbikes, like a gang of pizza delivery kids. The only cinema showed samurai movies, and there was an ice cream parlour on the plaza where they bought ice cream made from fruits with mysterious and resonant names: motojobobo, cacharana, pitanga, ocoró, asaí...

On her birthday, her parents took her to dinner at The Dragon Palace, the only Chinese restaurant in the area. There was a red and gold folding screen suspended from the ceiling, and the entrance was guarded by two stucco dragons. At the door, her parents respectfully greeted a blond man with puffy bags under his eyes: it was Señor T., who had once been a well-known singer. Now he was an alcoholic and sang in karaoke bars and at farmers' birthday parties. Señor T. greeted Ofelia's mother with an explosive kiss on the cheek that left her stunned and blushing. Then he gave Ofelia a birthday hug, enveloping her in his whisky breath: 'She's a pretty girl,' he said. 'Pity she didn't get her father's eyes.'

Before Ofelia's parents could react, Señor T. had walked off, and a waiter with a droopy false moustache and a red paper hat was leading them to a round table beside a tank in which stupefied catfish swam around and around. Ofelia's spirits had been dampened by the singer's remark. She couldn't cheer up even when they brought out the peach cake. After she'd blown out the candles, the waiter left them a tray of fortune cookies in foil wrappers with pictures of chrysanthemums. In the cookie that her older brother Mariano chose was the message: 'Superstition is the poetry of the poor.' Her mother got: 'Who is born an armadillo digs until his dying day,' which soured her mood. Ofelia's fortune cookie, on the other hand, came bearing promises: 'Wishes of all kinds fulfilled. Call 666-666.' She put the slip of paper in her pocket without showing it to anyone.

As she was falling asleep, thoughts jumped around in her head like monkeys in the treetops. She thought that she would have liked to be born with the green eyes of her father, the son of Italian farmers who had migrated, fleeing from war. But like her five siblings she'd ended up with the fiercely dark eyes of her mother, the ninth child of a hard-drinking country teacher and a woman from a dirt-poor family. Ofelia's mother had escaped the fate of her fellow villagers by marrying that handsome, green-eyed foreigner, and it was only because of her husband's business that she returned – she would never have looked back otherwise. When the village children asked Ofelia where she was from, she said without hesitation: Italy. In spite of the fact that she had never set foot in that country, and had inherited her Aunt Amanda's flat nose and just about everyone's dark-chocolate eyes.

The following day, in the house they were renting, she approached the mustard-coloured telephone, next to the black, leather-bound notebook in which her father kept the business cards of his clients and of the sawmills. Ofelia dialled the number on the slip of paper. Elevator music preceded the elegant diction of a secretary:

'How can I help you?'

That warm, modulated voice convinced her that it was a serious enterprise and not some kind of scam.

'It says in the advertisement that you fulfil wishes of all kinds. I want to have green eyes. Is that possible?'

'You need to discuss that in person with the Boss,' said the secretary.

Ofelia wrote down the address. She went there on Monday with a plastic purse containing the money that she had received for her birthday. The place turned out to be a tattoo parlour on the second storey of a covered market. There was a young metal-head in the waiting room, doing a crossword. The secretary was just as Ofelia had imagined her: incredibly pretty. Her paperweight was a crystal ball in which snow fell endlessly on a tiny house. When she looked up at Ofelia, her fake lashes rose like fans.

'The Boss is waiting for you,' she said.

When Ofelia went into the office, the Boss was hunched over the desk, inhaling a dust of fine crystals from a pocket mirror. He wiped his nose with the back of his hand, secreted the mirror in a drawer, and tidied his black hair, which was glossy with gel.

He had a dazzling white smile. Ofelia liked his close-fitting shirt, with its fine white, black and orange stripes, and sleeves rolled up to the elbows. It was a hot day, but the room was icy, although she couldn't see air-conditioning anywhere. There was a tropical picture on the wall: a toucan perched in a palm tree, the kind of thing junk dealers sell.

The Boss invited her to take a seat and looked her over from head to foot.

'I was starting to wonder what was taking you so long,' he said.

He brought his face close to Ofelia's: in the aroma that he gave off, there was a strong note of aniseed, which she found unpleasant. He enquired about her heart's desire. She whispered it into his ear, relieved to get it off her chest. The Boss nodded, unperturbed.

'Other girls have asked for stranger things,' he remarked.

She felt a tremendous sympathy for the Boss.

'How much does it cost?' she asked, nervously clutching her purse.

'All I need is a little signature.'

He placed a book in front of her: it was sturdily bound, and the pages were covered with the signatures of many other girls. Considering who he was, the Boss had surprisingly shaky hands and long, dirty fingernails, Ofelia thought. The scene was very familiar to her from the catechism books at school, and she was surprised how easy it was to give up the Kingdom of Heaven. Who cared about the choir of angels if she could have the mint-coloured eyes of her dreams...? She gripped the silver-plated pen firmly and inscribed her signature in large round letters: for the dot on the 'i', she drew a heart. She didn't feel anything out of the ordinary. Hardly anything, in fact: just the gentle flutter of memories escaping her, an incapacity to summon up the textures of jungle fruit and the faces of the village children, long-treasured images fading away, like the ribbon of starry sky between the branches of the trees ... But what is no longer remembered cannot be missed, and she was in a hurry to become someone else.

'Now look at me,' he said, as he lifted her chin.

Ofelia looked up to take in the world with her new eyes. She wanted to believe that the crude painting of the toucan would start to morph into the dreamed-of landscape of her father's homeland. But all she saw was the dark light emanating from the Boss's eyes as if spilling from an overturned jug.

Dazzled by her own reflection, she drew closer to give him a kiss.

The Narrow Way

The Devil can be a cloud, a shadow, a gust of wind that shakes the leaves. He can be the nightjar flying across the sky, or a reflection on the surface of the river. Some say he travels with the wind, others that he dwells in electricity. There are those who swear that he hides in the jungle, beyond the perimeter, where the branches whisper secrets that drive men crazy. But the Devil is also the scarecrow that runs across the fields when everyone is asleep.

'The World Outside is made of darkness,' says the Reverend, 'and whoever crosses the perimeter shall be swept away by the shadows. That is why we must not let ourselves be diverted from the narrow way, the way of our Lord. *Because strait is the gate, and narrow is the way, which leadeth unto life, and few there be that find it.*'

My sister Olga got tired of life on the narrow way. She and I used to sleep together, and sometimes, in the darkness, we'd play cows and calves. Susana, let's play cows and calves, she'd say, and lift up her nightie to offer me her tit. Her armpit hairs tickled my face like corn floss, and the inside of her arm smelled like warm ashes and bonfire smoke. I sucked on her tit as if I were the little calf Jacinta the cow had just dropped, and Olga had to cover her mouth so she wouldn't wake Father and Mother.

When people leave, they vanish into the shadows, Mother used to say. We never see them again, because we are the people of the narrow way, who work the earth and speak the name of God while waiting for the end of time. Here we conquer nature by the force of tractors and prayer, taming the wilderness, subjecting it to order. Beyond the perimeter lies the jungle with its shadows, and beyond that, the city with its illusions. If we are ever tempted to see what there is outside the colony, the obedience collar reminds us where we belong: at a distance of forty yards from the perimeter the current is a mere tickle, but as we approach the magnetic field, the shocks become more intense, more compelling, until we turn back to the way of the Lord.

The perimeter is our heritage, a reminder of our triumph over the world. But according to Olga, the adults made up those stories about the Outside just to scare us.

'There are no rivers of blood or flying letters or any of that stuff,' said Olga. 'For the people out there, we're the Outside. It's not like there are two skies; we're all the same, them and us and the animals.'

'Be quiet,' I replied.

The Devil gets into our thoughts, coiling up, spying, spinning his web. We were making marmalade in the kitchen: through the window, we could see Father unhitching the horse and unloading the gallons of herbicide he had bought in the city to spray on the cornfields. We wanted to see if the pockets of his overalls were bulging, because that was the sign that he had come back with delicious things we don't have in the colony, like locoto candies or liquid-centre bubblegum, but the only thing bulging in Father's overalls was his belly.

Olga spat into the pan of boiling marmalade for

the sheer pleasure of watching the phlegm dissolve slowly among the red bubbles. It wasn't for us, that marmalade: Father took it to the city when money was running short. Our spirits were weak: Olga and I dreamed of the city and everything that lay beyond the perimeter; we seized on snatches of music from vehicles driving past on the motorway and scoured the sky for aircraft, full of passengers, brushing the stars.

Mother had gone to the city once, many years earlier, not long after I was born. Whenever we asked her what it was like, she would suddenly go deaf. Mother, tell us what it's like. What did you see? What's there? Not a word. The men went to the city, though, with the Reverend's permission, to buy supplies, and sometimes they came back different, bareheaded, happier. That's why Olga spat in the marmalade: at least a part of her, she said, would leave the colony and travel to the city.

'I arranged to meet Jonas,' said Olga.

I went Shhhhh, because Father's ear was not far away.

Since we'd started meeting Jonas Feinman in the fields, Olga had changed. Jonas lived with his father and siblings in a house right near the perimeter, and when they were little, the Feinman brothers used to play with the magnetic field, approaching it to see who could stand the electric shocks the longest. Jonas's mother died of her last pregnancy: she put a knitting needle all the way in and scraped around inside until she bled to death. They didn't take her to the city to save her because she was damned already. People said it was hard for the Feinman children to keep to the narrow way because they had grown up without a mother; any distraction led them astray.

The tallest one, Jonas, began to take an unhealthy interest in the motorway. One night he heard laughter and voices, and climbed out of his bedroom window, barefoot. Beyond the perimeter he saw the blinking eyes of the motorbikes. The intruders had long hair and fingerless black leather gloves, and when they saw Jonas they whistled to him.

'Hey, come on over, nothing'll happen to you, we've got metamaterial,' they called out.

They spoke Bolivian, so Olga and I couldn't understand, but Jonas could because he was already old enough to go to the city with his father to buy seeds. The metamaterial came in a little box with a picture of a coiled-up snake on top. As well as deactivating the obedience collar, it interfered with the magnetic field, opening a breach in the perimeter. Through this gap, the size of a door, Jonas could cross to the other side without being electrocuted.

The young men provided safe conduct for dissidents. Their fathers had been fugitives, former followers of the narrow way who had escaped from the colony by digging a tunnel to the other side with the single-minded patience of a jungle armadillo, men who had betrayed the race by living with Bolivian women. It was forbidden to mention their sons. They were like us but different: they had broad cheeks and dark skin, but light eyes and long bones. They persuaded Jonas to ride pillion to the city, where people live in defiance of the Word, so that he could see for himself what it was like.

The dissidents brought him back to the colony at dawn and used their metamaterial to let him cross the perimeter. Soon he was back with the cows, milking, lugging hay, getting yelled at by old Feinman, who's famous for having kicked his horse to death one stormy night. But Jonas didn't care about the old man's bad temper, or the cows and their ticks, because he was still stunned, dazzled and thrilled by what he'd seen. From then on he started meeting the dissidents there on the boundary before midnight and returning in the early hours of the morning. Seeing him distracted, weary and yawning all day, old Feinman began to get riled up.

One Sunday after mass, Jonas took Olga and me to an abandoned stable to show us something. Ever since Olga's growth spurt and the appearance of her hips, men kept having something to show her. Jonas threatened to kill us if we told anyone.

'I'll cut your tongue out with a machete and give it to the pigs to eat,' he warned, but there was no need because simply being found with a boy would get you at least three days in the cage.

Jonas shifted a brick in the wall of the stable, reached into the hiding place, and took out a little metal ball that gave off a pink glow. The ball picked up the signal from Outside; the guys had given it to him so they could stay in touch. Fear rose out of the pit of my stomach, swirling weirdly. Jonas placed the metal ball on a brick; it began to wake up and blink and make a noise like boiling oil. Then the ball spoke with a woman's voice, hoarse and measured.

'What's it saying?' asked Olga.

But there was no time to reply. The voice fell suddenly silent and music burst out, made up of whistles and hisses, animal noises, ringing, things falling or rubbing together. We responded to the music with every bone in our bodies, vibrating inside as if we were made of echoes and tremors. I don't know how long we spent absorbing that poisoned rhythm, but that afternoon I understood why the metallic ball was the Devil's work.

Outside the abandoned stable, the wind combed miles of identical fields in one direction, blowing on them as if from a huge, angry mouth. Inside, Olga screamed with laughter, contorting herself.

'I'll show you how they dance in the city,' said Jonas, approaching my sister.

'Time is an illusion produced by the Devil,' said the Reverend. 'Centuries may go by Outside, but the time of the Lord is one and the same, and never passes.'

'Once when I was cleaning the roof, a bird came to visit,' said Jonas. 'It flew very high over the perimeter to get to me. I gave it some breadcrumbs to eat.'

'All the birds I come across have been electrocuted,' said Olga.

'OK, say "jukumari bear".'

'What kind of bear?'

'A kind there used to be.'

'What's it like riding a motorbike?' I wanted to know.

'Like flying.'

Rosie Fischer had a problem or a gift, depending on how you looked at it: her dreams came out of her head. Once she dreamed of a rhinoceros beetle: when she opened her eyes, the creature was crawling over her chest. One day she woke up screaming 'The ladder!' just as Klaus Ertland, who was climbing up to the roof to fix a solar panel, lost his footing, fell and broke his neck. Another time she dreamed of men with flags coming to check if we could read and knew the national anthem and swore allegiance to the country we'd never seen. By then Rosie's dreams were well known, and when the people from the government turned up at the colony we were ready and waiting with freshly baked cakes and the gift of a large suitcase. They opened the case, counted the bills, and left. They didn't come back.

We liked Rosie Fischer: her smell, her little blonde moustache, her broad back.

The three of us used to go and help the widow Elisabeth Kornmeier mend her children's clothes. Jacob Kornmeier had had the misfortune to die of a facial tumour, leaving his wife with eleven children, the youngest not yet weaned. The poor woman was very stupid; she never learned to cook or keep her house clean. When her children cried, she would cry along with them. The baby always had nappy rash. At the end of the afternoon, the widow would offer us cookies that were always hard and tasted of dirt, but we'd eat them without a word. We liked her. On the way home we looked for the baubles of the goldenberry hidden in the grass, played at spitting as far as we could, and ran around.

One time we spied on Daniel Wender when he was shitting in the field.

One time there was blood on my dress and I started crying because I thought I was going to die. It turned out I was a woman already. Olga and Rosie swore they wouldn't tell.

One time we saw the thing behind the shovel, in the barn, and the thing moved. Its legs were folded, it was squatting. It's a toad, said Rosie, who'd seen a picture of one in the book her grandfather kept hidden under his bed. The toad looked at us with its sad face, mildly surprised. We didn't know what to do with it, so we crushed it with the shovel.

One day Rosie dreamed that a beetroot had germinated inside her, a hard, red bulb. Soon it was clear that she was pregnant and nobody knew who the father was. It was the time of the high winds; the roof came off Aaron Weber's stable and blew away; the palm trees bent over so far their hair beat the ground.

The Reverend said: It's the Devil passing.

The widow Kornmeier's baby got colic, went red, and died. Gretel, her eighth daughter, said it was the widow's fault: she had breastfed after arguing with her oldest son and the bad milk had poisoned the baby. They buried him beside his father in a little box. It rained a lot that day. Everyone left a flower on the grave except for Rosie, who was nowhere to be seen.

That night Olga didn't want to go to sleep. Rosie's dream got her pregnant, she said, lying next to me, and when I came closer to suck her tit, she pushed me away. Don't you want to play cows and calves any more? Olga turned her back on me, anxiously pinching her arms to keep her eyes open, afraid of dreaming... of what? Children without fathers are leaves on the wind, not knowing who they are, where they come from, what carries them. They have to be given an anchor.

The Reverend said: Rosie will marry Abraham Jensen, and they went to fetch the little simpleton who talked to his shadow, and peed on himself when the bell rang.

Olga found Rosie's body near the perimeter on the way back from grinding corn. At first she thought it was a bundle of clothes that the wind had blown off the line and out to the edge of the colony. Then she noticed the smell of scorched flesh. When they managed to drag the body back with a shovel, they saw that the obedience collar had made Rosie's eyes pop out and left a black ring around her neck. The Reverend flatly refused to say a mass for Rosie or allow her to be buried in the cemetery. They threw her into the common grave, where Jonas Feinman's mother ended up, along with the dogs that nobody owned.

Olga and I kept going to the widow's place to mend clothes. But we no longer looked for fruit in the grass on the way back, or ran around, or felt like whistling.

To get over feeling sad about Rosie, Olga invented a game. You had to drink a glass of water, then another. And then, when the pressure in your bladder was becoming unbearable, you had to drink one more glass. After a while the tingling spread in painful waves and you had to contain it. Surround it with thought, concentrate it, rope it like a wild horse.

'Think of the centre,' said Olga, and the centre was a burning tip, a needle heated on an anvil. A lightning bolt.

'I can't think of anything.'

'Hold on a bit longer.'

She made me drink another glass. The rest of my body had gone numb. Just that instinctive retention. Then she tipped the contents of the jug into my lap. Between my legs the waters mixed, cold and warm.

And then the centre began to vibrate.

'God loves purity,' said the Reverend. 'Each kind with its own, no mixtures. Purity is perfection. Like attracts like.'

Our parents were married in accordance with this

teaching. Mother had turned fifteen. They were of the same blood. When the Reverend married them he said:

'God bless this union. From now on you are husband and wife. Previous bonds are dissolved. Share your happiness; may it be multiplied.'

They were in love; they wanted many children. Only Olga and I survived.

'The eye of the Lord has seen and He is angry,' repeated the Reverend as he walked up and down between the rows.

It was spiritual inspection day: chairs out in the churchyard, everyone present, no one speaking.

'Let the rot emerge into the light of day and dry out in the sun.'

The Reverend had X-ray eyes that could see right into us, all the way into the deepest recess where the secret lay buried. He shook a new metal rod over our heads.

'Let the evil in this community come forth.'

I was sitting next to Mother, looking down, with Olga right against me, rigid, struggling to keep what we had done from spilling out into the world. I said to my secret: 'Hide,' and my secret buried itself in the mud of my heart, and when the Reverend's white beard brushed me, I looked him in the face with my light eyes. Up close I could smell his rotten teeth. His eyes raked me with their fire and moved on.

Olga's secret had stayed hidden too.

I saw the widow Elisabeth Kornmeier looking restless. Suddenly she stood up and said: 'In my dreams I lie with a man who is not Jacob.' Then she collapsed.

In the row of men, Joshua Keppler, the giant, spoke:

'I secretly installed a water heater for the shower,' and he burst into tears.

Helmut Bauer confessed that he kept wine in his larder. And so the sins leaped into the Reverend's net as one sinner after another broke down.

Sitting beside old Feinman, Jonas opened his mouth. What will come out? I wondered, tense on my chair. Olga beside me was pale. What will his open mouth say? What came out was a bold, luxurious yawn. His father punched him in the face:

'Shut it, you brute,' he said. 'Have some respect.'

Blood spurted from Jonas's nose and ran down all over his mouth. The Reverend pretended not to have seen.

Passing over our heads, the Reverend's rod made a beeping sound whenever it detected anything metallic, and the guilty had no choice but to show what they were hiding: electric razors, miniballs for connecting with the Outside, implants. We gazed at all these objects with fear and desire.

The sinners were taken to the cages, which were tall enough to allow for standing prayer. Each penitent entered without complaint, and the Reverend put on the locks. They stayed there for ten days to feed the mosquitoes and learn a lesson. By the end, Elisabeth Kornmeier's hair had gone completely white.

And the Reverend said with satisfaction:

'The source has been cleansed, the impurity washed away.'

But the next day we got dirty again.

We went back to the stable to feel the music. It was raining. The sky was electric, gashed with lightning that lit up one cornfield, then another. Thunder boomed.

Jonas's nose was crooked from the punch; that was just how his face would look now. He rolled the metal ball in the palm of his hand. The music bounced off the walls. A lightning flash: Olga lifted up her skirt, giggled, spun around. Another flash: Jonas chased Olga and threw her to the ground. She dug her fingernails into his face, laughing uncontrollably. They had forgotten about me. They wrestled in the shadows. The ball was rolling on the floor, and the voice spoke in our language: You're listening to Dissident Radio.

I felt sad. The world had never seemed so big.

'Jonas,' said Olga in the darkness, and she laughed.

We returned to the widow's house once more. We found her sitting with a bundle in her arms. She was singing a lullaby.

The bloodthirsty spider spun a sticky trap. A fly came flying by and got stuck in the web.

She had opened all the windows. The cotton curtains were billowing in the breeze. It was like everything was levitating. Her four-year-old son was crying on the floor, beside a broken cup, the palm of his hand red with blood.

The widow smiled as she sang. She held the baby's shroud to her chest; there was dirt on her hands and her clothes.

The little fly was struggling, tangled in the web; the bloodthirsty spider came and ate it up.

'Elisabeth Kornmeier,' said my sister. 'What's wrong?'

The white hair made her look like an old woman.

'Elisabeth Kornmeier!'

I dreamed of an armadillo stopped in the middle of the path. Everything was still, alert and shining; not a leaf stirred. Behind the armadillo was the tunnel it had dug, little by little, day by day. The armadillo's tunnel went down to the depths of the earth.

I opened my eyes. It was night. Olga was sitting on the edge of the bed, coiling her braids up on top of her head. Jonas's silhouette was peering in through the window. It was like what happened with Rosie Fischer: a dream had escaped from my head, flown out of me into the world.

If I'd reached out I could have touched Olga. But I didn't move. Father and Mother were snoring in the next room; all I had to do was say something. I pretended to be asleep. Olga laced up her boots.

'I know you're awake,' said Olga, with her back to me. 'Don't try to find me, pretend I'm dead.'

Without looking back, she ran off through the corn, towards the roaring motors and the electricity.

I stayed awake: Olga's laughter was shaking the fields.

You Glow in the Dark

They put us all in the Olympic Stadium. The neighbourhood was deserted, the doors of the houses left open, meals still warm on the tables, dogs howling in gardens for their owners. They kept us for hours without telling us anything. I was very scared to be close to so many people; God forgive me but even the children frightened me; I didn't want them anywhere near me with those dirty little hands of theirs, those innocent, possibly lethal hands. No one knew where the poison was lurking, in what part of the body or the clothing. They made us line up and the checking began.

Most of all, they inspected our feet: if the detector started beeping, they ordered you to wash yourself over and over with coconut soap and vinegar until your skin was red like urucú pods from all the scrubbing. They didn't find anything on me, or my mother, or my sister Ana Lúcia, or my uncle Silas, or even my cousin Gislene, who's always in and out of bars, rubbing up against men, but on my father they did. My poor father had gone to have a few drinks with the owner of the scrapyard, who lived nearby. And because he spent an hour at the scrap dealer's place and got contaminated with that stuff, which is finer than sand and made of fire, they evacuated us all and demolished our house: they didn't let us take a single family photo, or heirloom, or piece of clothing. My father had just retired from his job as an usher at the Goiânia Theatre so he could make the most of his house and garden. And from one day to the next, the house was gone. Not one brick left. Absolutely nothing.

One day Mr Atílio, the owner of the bakery, ran into my father on the bus and started talking loudly, so everyone could hear, about how Dad was one of the sufferers, such a terrible thing, so dangerous. Right away the passengers started yelling and staring at my father with disgust and terror in their eyes, as if they'd come across a coiled viper, a hairy spider or a dead rat full of maggots, and eventually the driver pulled over and kicked Dad off the bus for having caused a ruckus on public transport. The government gave us a house in a different part of the city, where nobody knew us, but my father never got over the trauma of that incident on the bus. He died two months later, supposedly of kidney failure caused by his drinking, but I think it was the little grain of fire. People we knew began to die of rare and aggressive diseases.

At the time, I was working as a receptionist at Castro's Park Hotel, the one that's fifteen storeys high and has two tiled swimming pools. I liked that job. At the time of the accident, the Grand Prix was being held in the city for the first time, and the international teams were staying at the hotel. One of the drivers told me there was a rumour going around that something terrible was happening in Goiânia and the race could be called off at any moment. He was really handsome, with slicked-back hair and a gold cross on a fine chain around his neck. Before going off he asked for my telephone number and gave me a pack of menthol cigarettes, which my cousin took from my bedside table, because I don't smoke.

I never knew if he'd tried to call: a few days later I was homeless, living with my family in a tent. Anyway, once the rumour got going, panic spread, and from one day to the next, the hotel was empty. No one wanted to come to the city any more, for any reason. Whenever the phone rang it was people cancelling reservations, and the hotel had a sad feeling all the time. One day the manager called me to his office and fired me. The end of 1987, that was: I had just turned nineteen, and my father was already in the ground. That's how I ended up running off to São Paolo with a friend, although we didn't know anyone there.

When we arrived, we nearly got jobs at a jeweller's in Rua Barão de Paranapiacaba. It was a few days before Christmas, and the street was sparkling with little lights and tinsel. But as soon as the owner found out we were from Goiânia, she made up excuses and wouldn't take us on. As we were about to step into the street, she called out to us. For a moment we thought she might have changed her mind. The woman's curiosity was piqued. There was something she just had to ask:

'Do you glow in the dark?'

*

*** THE SCRAP HUB ***
SCRAP METAL OF ALL KINDS BOUGHT
AND SOLD
TELEPHONE: 233-9269

The scrap collectors brought their cart piled high with pieces of metal; they told him it came from the abandoned clinic on the corner of Paranaíba and Tocantins Avenues, in the Airport District. Devair remembered the hospital: years earlier he'd seen the doctors going in and out, and the people lining up for cancer treatment. The building had been a ruin for some time. One wing had been demolished. The part left standing had no roof or windows, so the collectors hadn't expected to find the furniture and medical equipment still in place. What kind of people could afford to walk away from a hospital and leave all the equipment inside? they said.

Devair didn't care where the scrap came from: people brought him car parts, old TVs, worn-out pots and pans, bike handlebars, stolen goods. The load weighed nine hundred pounds. He offered the men fifteen hundred cruzeiros and they took it without haggling: they were heading straight to the bar to treat their headaches with a few drinks. He noticed the men's weird tan – a deep orange shade – but said nothing; there were stranger things to be seen all the time in the neighbourhood.

The light took him by surprise that night when he was smoking in the garden, beside the corrugated iron lean-to. It was coming from inside the heap of scrap that he had just bought, fading to a milky, iridescent veil of varying shades: a blue luminescence as if from a star or the depths of the sea. He was afraid. He thought of the dead, of the Devil, of aliens.

He prised the pieces of metal apart and traced the glow to a cylinder the size of a thimble: a treasure in the midst of the junk. Turning it over, he discovered that the light shone out only when the source was in line with a tiny window: now you see it, now you don't, like a magic trick.

He sat down in the corner where he took appliances apart, under the lamp, with all his tools around him – the big wrench and the little one, the hammer, the set of screwdrivers, the ratchet wrench, the drill, the pliers, the pincers, the hacksaw with its broken, rusty blade – and jabbed at the peephole several times with the tip of a screwdriver. With a faint crack, the little window broke open. He dug around in the eye of the capsule and finally extracted a couple of grains on the tip of the screwdriver: in the beam of the lamp, they looked like some kind of ordinary mineral salt, nothing special. Could those little grains have been the source of the light?

He switched off the lamp. In the dark, as he suspected, the salt became an incandescent snow. He rubbed at that substance and the glow spread over the palm of his hand. Awed and puzzled, he observed the celestial combustion. There, between the blue glow and the shadows of the scrap metal behind him, an idea began to emerge in his brain like the head of a mushroom pushing up after showers. He would make a gift for his wife: the most beautiful, shimmering, unusual ring. He smiled.

*

I was in Goiânia for a government project when I got the call. It was the director of the hospital to tell me that in the previous days they'd admitted various patients suffering from an unidentified illness: the symptoms were vomiting, dizziness, diarrhoea and burns. He said people were blaming a metal tube, a demonic piece of steel that the scrap dealer's wife had brought in. And where is ... ? I asked him. In one of the offices, said the director, cutting me off. You mean the woman? I asked. No, the metal tube, he said. I don't know where the woman is. And then he added: Do you think it's possible ... ? He sounded uneasy, afraid of making a fool of himself. Those people, you know, they're ignorant, they make up all sorts of stuff, he said. He wanted to be reassured, to be told: Don't worry, it's nothing. I'd worked with a uranium prospecting outfit near the Amorinópolis volcano the previous year, so I called them to see if I could borrow a detector. The secretary remembered me warmly; in fact, she didn't even ask me to sign for it.

When I got to the hospital, there were two firemen sitting on the pavement next to their truck, smoking and telling jokes. A nurse pointed the way to the office where they had put the piece of metal. The corridor leading to that office was full of patients: pregnant women, babies, old crocks. About two hundred and fifty feet from the office, the detector started behaving very strangely: the needle jumped so wildly I thought there must have been a fault. I came back to the hospital with another detector. Again, two hundred and fifty feet from that room, the detector reached saturation. That could only mean two things. Either both detectors were faulty or the hospital was a dirty bomb.

One of the firemen went into the office and came out with a bag: he smiled at me as if he was carrying a ham sandwich. It was the nylon bag they had stored the piece of metal in. He wasn't even wearing gloves: that was when I realised that this fireman was little more than a boy. I asked him what he was doing. I'm going to throw it in the river, he said. The hospital secretary had a transistor radio: she looked at me dreamily, tapping her lacquered nails in time with a Cazuza song. I heard myself yell FOR THE LOVE OF GOD! My voice was the shriek, the screech, the squawk of a scared, ridiculous bird.

We evacuated the health centre immediately.

*

Devair didn't know what it was for, the dust he had found in the cylinder, which shone all night long at the foot of his bed. His wife Gabriela complained that the glow gave her headaches and really weird dreams; her lack of enthusiasm annoyed him, but that would change, he thought, when he presented her with the luminous ring. He had to get more of the substance out, and to do that he had to break the capsule's protective outer shell. His employees at the scrap yard, Israel and Admilson, took turns pounding the device first with a hammer, then with a sledgehammer until they cracked it open – it wasn't too hard; they were young and strong. (The following month both would be well and truly dead and buried, in lead-lined coffins under a cement slab. Transferred by helicopter, against his will, to the Naval Hospital in Rio de Janeiro, Admilson would cry his mother's name over and over as he lay dying.)

Devair summoned friends, relatives and neighbours, and distributed the miracle of the fluorescent salts. His pal Marcio put his share in a pocket and later scattered it in the farmyard, causing commotion among the chickens and pigs. Mr Ernesto gave the grains to his wife, who, angry that he'd come home drunk, threw the powder down the toilet without even looking at it. Claudio thought it might have been some kind of gunpowder invented by the army, and tried to ignite it with his lighter, but the salts didn't burn or melt. Ivo, his brother, took a few granules to paint the little body of Leide das Neves with light. The magic dust delighted the girl: she sat down to dinner with sparkly particles all over her hands.

The only one who didn't join in the celebrations was Gabriela. She was wary, impatient, suspicious of so much glee. Like a dog that sniffs a storm on the air, like a bird that hears a shot on the far side of the forest, her whole body was picking up the danger signals.

*

Some said it was a bad feijão. Some said it was sunstroke. Others remembered the sewage seething with mosquitoes and called the Institute of Tropical Diseases. Someone said it was Dona Lena, the santera who lived in a flimsy stick hut, and a group of people wanted to go and set her shack on fire. This is what comes of drinking till dawn, said the wife of one of the men. It's an excuse they invented to get out of coming to work, said the owner of a factory. Plenty of rest, said the doctor.

Gabriela was awake all night with a high fever, thinking, brooding. She thought about when she was seven and saw the sea for the first time, in Paraíba, after a three-day journey with her father: the amazement that rushed in through her mouth and was so big it hurt. She thought about how they'd slept in hammocks right beside the sea. She thought about how her father went from village to village selling hammocks, and carried her strapped to his back, how he spoon-fed her things she didn't like (beetroot, sardines, cauliflower), and the wild pigs they'd seen running in the plaza in Belém do Brejo do Cruz, and the thunderstorm that had surprised them one night when they were sleeping out in the open. She thought about the day when her father said: Wait for me here, and didn't come back, and she stood there on that corner until darkness fell, and never saw her father again – she could barely remember his beard and the anchor tattoo that said God loves you (and she thought about all the times she'd looked for that tattoo on other men's bodies). She thought about what it was like to be hungry, and scared, and cold, about the women with red sequins and long legs who called her honey. She thought about when she used to wear a ribbon in her hair and work in the pharmacy in Espírito Santo, and the man who came in to ask for throat lozenges, and how he looked at her, and the anchor tattoo just up from his wrist. She thought about how she'd told him: I'm fourteen, and about his daughter, who was almost her age and had a name she thought was pretty: Dione. She thought about the pharmacist who treated her after what happened happened and said: Forget about having children. She thought about the blood, the fear of dying and the wanting to die. About how the lightning struck just a few yards from the tree where she and her father were sheltering that stormy night, and that blue light you could see with closed eyes, which had stayed with her, trapped in her head all through those quiet, calm, happy years with Devair. She thought about how all she'd ever done was wait for the return of that light, which was the light of the Devil.

By the time the dawn filtered in through the curtains, she had made up her mind. She rose without making a sound, still trembling with fever, and got herself ready to leave: a lock of black hair came out, tangled in the teeth of the comb. Devair was tossing and turning in bed, his face creased in an anxious frown and stained that unreal orange colour it had taken on in the last few days. She silently begged his forgiveness for what she was about to do. Repressing the urge to throw up, she put the cylinder in a bag and set out for the hospital.

*

STATE ATTORNEY'S OFFICE, GOIÁS, 30 NOV, 1987
POLICE INVESTIGATION NO. 54 / 87

The Goiânia Radiotherapy Institute was established on 2 May, 1972, and in 1974 it obtained a licence from the National Nuclear Energy Commission (CNEN) for the use of radioactive material, in this case a caesium 137 source, model CESAPAN F-3000, made in Italy (marketed by Generay). Subsequently the Institute sought authorisation to use a cobalt-60 source, Generay model Jupiter Jr. II.

When the Goiânia Radiotherapy Institute (IGR) moved its headquarters to No. 305, Rua 1-A, Airport District, in the midst of a legal dispute, the owners of the Institute took the cobalt source and left the caesium source at the former hospital on the Avenida Paranaíba. One of the owners, Doctor Amaurillo Monteiro de Oliveira, hired builders to remove the tiles, windows, doors and other materials from the building, leaving the premises completely unprotected and accessible to anyone who wished to enter.

According to the investigation, the doctors and owners of the company were aware that the source was highly dangerous, but chose to leave it behind and not to inform the National Nuclear Energy Commission at any point that they were vacating the facilities on Avenida Paranaíba. The caesium source had been abandoned for three years when it was found by the scrap collectors Wagner Mota Pereira, aged nineteen, and Roberto dos Santos Alves, aged twenty-two.

*

NUCLEAR CEMETERY, ABADIA DE GOIÁS, 2021

Kamilinha, Leide das Neves's favourite doll, is buried in drum #305. In #2897 are the remains of Titã, Mr Ernesto's dog. In #1758, all the photos of the Alves Ferreira family. The branches of the mango tree from the house of Roberto dos Santos Alves are to be found in drum #65. Drum #3007 contains the remains of Marcio's chickens. Drum #2503 is full of chunks of tarmac from Rua 57. Gislene's diary, with a list of all her lovers from 1982 to 1987, is in drum #13. Drum #492 holds Devair's tools. In drum #666 there are unused rolls of toilet paper. Lourdes das Neves's favourite dress, in blue satin with yellow flowers, is in drum #27. Receptacle #1234 contains a letter that Israel never sent to his ex-girlfriend, the only letter he ever wrote. The clothes that Gabriela Ferreira wore in hospital as she lay dying were thrown into drum #78. Drum #75 holds bottles of Brahma beer from the bar on Rua 26-A, many unopened. Drum #789 is empty: the workers made a mistake. Two tickets for the film *E.T.* are hidden in drum #89. In drum #1894 is an unopened box of Garoto chocolates that Luiza Odet had just bought at the supermarket. An ID card belonging to Admilson's brother, who disappeared during the dictatorship, is in drum #2406. In drum #785 is a poem written on a napkin:

```
                        st air st air st air
                     st air st air st air
                  st air st air st air
               st air st air st air
            st air st air st air
         st air st air st air
```

*

PHOTOGRAPHIC TOUR OF ABADIA
DE GOIÁS
—
THE MORNING PAPER

In 1952 the cowhand Paulino Inácio Rosa, his wife Salma Jorge Rosa and their two children built the first house in what was still a rural area, fifteen miles from Goiânia. One of the children, Inácio, better known as Badico, fell seriously ill and had to undergo complicated spinal surgery in Rio de Janeiro. Salma Jorge Rosa promised to erect a chapel for the adoration of the Virgin if Badico was able to walk again.

The church with its image of Our Lady of Abadia was consecrated ten years later, and the locality, where more and more people were settling, came to be known as Abadia de Goiás. The first petrol station was set up by Dorivaldo – better known as Dori – who sold it right away to Gorgonio – Nego Forte, as everyone called him – who extended the building and turned it into the Nego Forte steak house, which is still going today.

The nuclear cemetery is barely more than half a mile from the edge of town, on a plot of land guarded twenty-four hours a day by the Military Police Battalion for Protection of the Environment. At this site, 40,000 of radioactive waste are stored in 3,800 metal drums, which are kept in a concrete vault between two banks of earth covered with sun-scorched grass.

The cemetery was supposed to be a temporary solution to an unprecedented problem. But for years now the inhabitants of Abadia de Goiás have been demanding in vain the transfer of the toxic material to some other part of Brazil. The fact is, no one wants the nuclear waste. The initial idea of burying it under an air force base in the Amazon was abandoned after protests by the local indigenous people, and no other state is prepared to take charge of such a hazardous can of worms.

In 1995, protesting against the nuclear cemetery that had been imposed upon them, the inhabitants of Abadia de Goiás decided to break away and form their own mini-municipality. But the problem is not about to disappear: the dump will remain radioactive for the next three hundred years.

*

The year of the accident I was pregnant with my second daughter, living one hundred and fifty yards from Devair's junkyard in Rua 26-A. We were in and out of the prohibited area all the time: people used those streets to get to work and back; journalists visited the houses to interview those who'd been exposed; children secretly played in the contaminated zone. I was so naive I stayed and had my daughter there.

I stopped thinking about what had happened. The city grew very quickly, sprouting condos and new neighbourhoods, filling up with people who brought their whole families from Bahia or Maranhão and didn't care what had gone on. The thing is, we were just coming out of a dictatorship: we had been trained to forget. My daughters grew up; I discovered boxing at forty-plus, started training at a gym in the Airport District, and then competing in regional championships. One day I went down Rua 57 and saw some street art on a wall. It was just a picture, no words, but when I saw it, the whole story came back to me – every detail.

That unsigned mural on the wall of a ruin seemed to be talking back to the present. I stared at it so long, amazed by what I could remember, I ended up missing my bus. I walked home, thinking, arguing with myself, and when I got back I examined my younger daughter from her ears down to the tips of her toes, searching for the fault, the defect. She wanted to know what was wrong with me, why I'd suddenly gone crazy: she'd never understand.

The next time after training, I stopped in Rua 57 to try and find out more about the mural: no one could tell me who had painted it or how long it had been there. A neighbour said the building had been vacant and abandoned for many years: kids got in there at night to listen to music and take drugs. Maybe they'd done the painting, he suggested. I roamed all over Goiânia looking for similar street art, but couldn't find any. Where the Goiânia Radiotherapy Institute had been, there was a huge, showy convention centre. And not a single plaque in the whole city to explain what had happened.

One afternoon, walking home from the gym, I had a strange feeling that made me stop. At first, I didn't know what it was, I just had the impression that something was missing or out of place. Then I saw it. The wall. The mural in Rua 57 wasn't there. It had been covered by a thick layer of still-wet paint. The colour white had never seemed so bright and sinister. A woman sweeping in front of her door noticed my puzzlement. At last the council covered up that awful monstrosity, she said with satisfaction. Apparently there's going to be a beauty salon there.

*

The band is called Radioactive Flesh. Zé Maconha is the drummer, Suicide Girl plays bass, I'm on guitar, and my girlfriend sings back-up. We're all from Jardim Novo Mundo, we only play in contaminated areas and choose the venue the night before. None of our parents own a home. Thirty people showed up at the first gig, at the next one there were fifty, now there's more than a hundred of us. Are we afraid of cancer? Listen, the police are going to take us out before the cancer does.

*

One day our little pig went missing. Dedé forgot to close the garden gate, and Lampião saw his chance and ran off into the night. We were really sad. We had raised that piglet ourselves; on cold days my wife used to wrap him in a scarf. We cried, thinking he might have been killed. Someone came to the house. They said: Why don't you pray to the little saint? She works miracles. The carpenter's wife, who couldn't get pregnant, gave birth to a healthy baby girl after leaving her an offering. My wife: And who's this saint? That someone: Leide das Neves, a powerful little saint because she died as a child without having sinned. She was the niece of that man Devair, who ruined his family and his neighbours with the poisonous light. The poor girl died all busted up. My wife: Is this some kind of Macumba thing? That one: She's buried in Christian soil, out in the Parque cemetery. At the time of her death, a crowd gathered to stop her burial, scared she would contaminate the cemetery; they even threw stones at her. The girl's tomb was vandalised. But over time people came to see that she was working miracles, and now there are always flowers and candles and thank you cards beside the gravestone. We hesitated but we really needed help. My wife went out to the cemetery with a pair of blessed candles. And that afternoon the son of a neighbour turned up with Lampião in his arms. He said he'd found him eating grass on the football field, calm as you please. We checked the piglet over: not a scratch. Hallelujah! said my wife. And she kneeled down to thank the little saint for her mercy.

*

To get to the house you had to cross a ruined patio several yards deep; the potholes in the tarmac were swarming with tadpoles. It was the last house, almost hidden behind two mango trees, which cast their shadows into the street. A woman was charging for entry, and a boy guided people to the back garden, where a sheet of blue plastic offered protection from the imminent rain. The chickens kept getting under the visitors' feet.

Devair was seated in the middle of the garden, hanging his head, sleepy, very drunk. And beside him, the presenter in a suit, who said:

Ladies and gentlemen, this man survived the radiation, the burns, the deaths, the dishonour and the tragedy. He lost his wife, his niece, his business, his employees, his family, his hair and his friends, but, viewers, he did not lose his dignity.

The power of God is great, someone yelled.

This man did not die, the presenter went on. He is alive by the grace of God, to the amazement of mankind. Ladies and gentlemen, you are about to witness a wonder without equal. This man came into contact with death, with malignity, with the radiant Devil. What is the body but that which breathes? Open your eyes, ladies and gentlemen, what you are about to see is not for the fainthearted: the glow of death, the phosphorescence of sin, the man who shines in the darkness.

The boy stood on tiptoe to get a better view, and the presenter went to switch off the lights. Drunk and oblivious to the crowd he had drawn, Devair snored.

※

Note

Although the events narrated in 'You Glow in the Dark' are based on the Goiânia radiological accident of 1987, the story is a work of fiction. The 'stair' poem quoted is by Ronald Johnson, from his book *Songs of the Earth*.

The Aura Estrada Prize allowed me to take up residencies at Oax-i-fornia (Oaxaca), Art Omi (Ghent, New York) and the Ucross Foundation (Wyoming). Spending time in those places helped me to develop the ideas for a number of the stories in this book.

The participants in the Sunday workshops in Ithaca commented on different versions of some of the stories: Janet Hendrickson, Francisco Díaz Klaassen, Eliana Hernández, Sebastián Antezana, Paulo Lorca, Giovanna Rivero, Juliana Torres, Isabel Calderón and Roberto Ibáñez. Thanks also to Edmundo Paz Soldán, Juan Cárdenas, Martín Felipe Castagnet, Alexis Argüello, Mónica Heinrich, Juan Pablo Piñeiro, Mariano Vespa, Adhemar Manjón, Juan Casamayor and Chris Andrews for their reading. And to Gabriel Mamani for the photo of the mural in Goiânia.

I thank Laurence Laluyaux for her support and enthusiasm.

Also translated by Chris Andrews

A Bookshop in Algiers, Kaouther Adimi, Serpent's Tail

The Wind that Lays Waste, Selva Almada, Charco

The Lime Tree, César Aira, And Other Stories

Amulet, Roberto Bolaño, Vintage Classics

I Don't Care, Ágota Kristóf, New Directions

Coming soon from Akoya

FICTION

My Clavicle and Other Massive Misalignments, Marta Sanz

they, Helle Helle

The Oldest Bitch Alive, Morgan Day

Chiquitita, Pedro Carmona-Alvarez

La Playa, Marina Perezagua

NON-FICTION

Glimmer, Ilona Wiśniewska

POETRY

Horses, Jake Skeets

akoya
An Independent Publishing House

Akoya celebrates courageous, visionary and innovative writing from around the world.

We are a home for authors and translators, not just their books.

Discover more from Akoya at

www.akoyapublishing.com
@akoyapublishing

Akoya Publishing
222 Kensal Road, London, W10 5BN

Copyright © Liliana Colanzi, 2022
First published in Spanish as *Ustedes brillan en lo oscuro*
by Editorial Páginas de Espuma
English language copyright © Chris Andrews, 2024
First published in the English language in the USA
by New Directions in 2024
First published in the English language in the UK
by Akoya Publishing in 2025

The right of Liliana Colanzi to be identified as the
author of this work has been asserted by her in
accordance with Section 77 of the Copyright, Designs
and Patents Act 1988

The right of Chris Andrews to be identified as the
translator of this work into the English language has
been asserted by him in accordance with Section 77 of
the Copyright, Designs and Patents Act 1988

Paperback ISBN 978-1-83675-004-8
Ebook ISBN 978-1-83675-011-6

This is a work of fiction. All characters, organisations
and events are purely the product of the author's
imagination and used fictitiously.

Design by Holly Titchener
Text design by Phil Cleaver
Typeset in 10/13pt Egizio URW by Six Red Marbles UK,
Thetford, Norfolk
Printed and bound in the UK by CPI Group (UK) Ltd,
Croydon, CR0 4YY

1 3 5 7 9 10 8 6 4 2

All rights reserved. No part of this publication may
be reproduced, stored or transmitted in any form
or by any means without prior written permission
from the publisher.

A CIP record for this book is available from
the British Library.

akoyapublishing.com